Badge of Loyalty

Jude Tresswell

First published 2018
by Rowanvale Books Ltd
The Gate
Keppoch Street
Roath
Cardiff
CF24 3JW
www.rowanvalebooks.com

A CIP catalogue record for this book is available from the British Library.
ISBN: 978-1-911569-54-1

Contents

Chapter 1

Phil

There's an Irish song about an angel that loved a human. I don't know anything about the deity the angel worked for, other than it was a bloody cruel one. It stripped the angel of its wings. I like to think that they were rainbow coloured.

The problem was, the angel wasn't meant to love the clay. What happens, though, when the clay loves the angel? That song is still playing.

The painting I'm looking at isn't a typical Raith Balan. It's a scene in a leafy garden. As such, it's markedly different from the wild waterfalls Raith paints for his own satisfaction and from the erotic ceramics that he sculpts primarily for the pleasure of others.

There are four men seated round a pub-style table, a parasol advertising lager unsuccessfully staving off the heat; all four men look hot. Raith himself sits on the left. He's leaning forward, talking urgently with animation. Obviously, one can't infer that from the painting. Though Raith's work is admirable—or so they tell me, anyway—he hasn't managed to make it speak yet, other than to the emotions, of course! But I know, because I'm the figure on the right holding a half-empty bottle of brown ale. Probably brown ale. Raith remembers the details of that day in the garden with greater clarity than I do. But then, Raith can recall most things he sees, and his hand can reproduce exactly what is held in his memory.

Ross is seated between us, worry adding to his thirty-something years. You can see the concern in the knit of his eyebrows and in the tightness of the muscles in his neck and bare arms. Concern for the fourth man, whose face Raith has never painted. Mike Angells, the man all three of us love and who, somehow, manages to love all three of us. Raith and I both know that we aren't the ones he'd risk his life for, though. If only Ross had had a different surname, not one named after a town in north-east England. Whitburn-Howe. That's Ross's surname. He usually only uses the 'Whitburn', and that was the part that caused us so much trouble. Within bell-ringing distance of Sunderland, and it rang one bell too many for our comfort.

* * *

"Anybody we know being reinflicted on society this week, Ron?" asked Superintendent Flaxby.

"One we might want to keep an eye on, yes," Detective Chief Inspector Fortune replied. "Remember seven years ago, that shooting at Merton's warehouse on Cantrill Industrial Estate?"

"I certainly do. The Babcock brothers. Angells' case."

"That's the one. Luke Babcock got sent down for ten years, along with his brother, but he's being let out early. The brother's got another year to do."

The super nodded. "I'll worry more this time next year when the two of them are running round loose again," he said phlegmatically.

"One for the inspector to lose a bit of sleep about, I'd have thought, though," said the DCI.

Flaxby could almost hear the glee in the chief

inspector's voice as he offered his news. Luke Babcock had always maintained that he was merely a bystander, innocently caught up in a vicious attack on a warehouse security guard. According to his lawyer, he'd even tried to stop the attack. The judge had had none of it. Angells' case was technically sound and the evidence was watertight, so Babcock had been led away swearing not-so-sweet revenge.

"Does he know?" asked Flaxby.

"Not yet. I was going to tell him when he came in."

I bet you were, thought Flaxby.

"I need to see him anyway. I'll tell him myself," he said aloud, adding, too quietly for Fortune to hear him, "I'm not giving you the pleasure, you jealous sod."

The first thing Flaxby did when he got into his office was telephone the governor at Blay Fenn Prison. Ten minutes later, he felt fairly reassured. If Babcock did have thoughts of retribution, he hadn't been voicing them recently. But then, you never knew, and for that very reason, you couldn't allow yourself to worry much. For Angells' sake, though, he'd have liked to have had the bastard watched for a week and, hopefully, seen him off his turf; but cuts were cuts, and he didn't have the officers to sort out the urgent tasks clogging up his in-tray, his desk, his chairs, his room... let alone the non-essential ones.

It would probably be all right. The badge was a great protector. Anyway, there were more pressing things to think about. So he left a message on Inspector Angells' desk. *See me when you get in.*

Mike Angells, pronounced with a hard 'g' like go and get. Not that hard 'g's meant anything to Raith, who habitually addressed most folk as 'babe' and, knowing an angel when he saw one, preferred to call all five foot eleven of Mike his 'Angel Baby'. At work, his nicknames were less flattering. As long as the super was out of earshot, Ron Fortune called him 'Angela'. Mike always ignored the provocation—a wise move, as Detective Chief Inspector Fortune was his immediate superior in the Tees, Tyne and Wear CID.

Fortune and Angells disliked and distrusted each other, but while Mike had the self-discipline, respectfulness and courtesy to subjugate personal dislike to professionalism, Fortune had no such scruples.

Suspicious of those he still referred to as poofs and queers, and most definitely not the face of modern policing, he envied his younger colleague's standing with the super. Fortune was furious to think that, with the upper echelons bending over backwards to nail their rainbow colours to the mast, kowtowing to the law if not to the zeitgeist, he would find his path to superintendent blocked, whereas 'a fucking sodomite like Angela' would doubtless make it sooner or later. Probably sooner: he was rising steadily. So Fortune made sure that, if he had to be ordered around by a fucking fairy in the future, he'd order the slack-arse around now.

Flaxby knew all this, and would have liked to have Fortune transferred, but in a shrinking force, with recruitment at an all-time low and experienced cops retiring early, he needed all the skill and knowledge he could get to keep his Warbridge division running smoothly. So, he deflected the slings and arrows whenever he was able to, and it was he, not Fortune, who requested Angells' presence on that particular morning.

There was a knock on Flaxby's office door, and Angells pushed the door open.

"You wanted me, sir?"

"Come in. Sit down, man."

Flaxby waited until Angells had deposited the pile of paperwork that took up both available chairs onto just one of them.

"Do you want me to take some of this stuff off you, sir?" he asked, sitting down.

"You mean you've nothing better to do, Mike?" Flaxby said, smiling.

"Wouldn't go as far as that. If it helps, though."

"No, but thanks. Something's come up. Mike, what's the word on the street about these farm machinery thefts?"

"Not being funny, sir, but would that be on the street in general, or are you specifyin' my Street and gossip at the Tunhope Arms?"

The stretch of narrow, winding road that ran from Tunhope on the 689 through to Tunhead at the head of Tun Beck was called 'The Street', and the Arms was the only pub for miles. Thus it was the inspector's local, if a local can be three miles away from home as the crow flies and ten if you stick to poorly maintained tarmac.

"Your Street. Much being said?"

"I'd say the farmers are worried, sir. We've had nuthin' taken up the Tun yet, but the farms to the east of ours have been hit and that's gettin' too close for comfort."

"What sort of stuff's going?"

"Old stuff, as far as I know. The only kind of machinery these hill farmers have. They can't afford all the new gear. If the goods are endin' up abroad, which is what the thinkin' is, the thieves want the old stuff. Mechanics not electronics. Things you can fix with a screwdriver and a bit of gaffer tape, not a load of fancy engine management linked to a computer. There's quads gone too, though," he added. "At least three that I know of, and that hits these farmers really hard."

"What's security like?" the super inquired.

"Well, non-existent usually," the inspector replied. "There's all this advice goin' around from us and from the insurance companies—perimeter fencin', CCTV, security lightin'—but it costs an arm and a leg. Mostly, the farms rely on their dogs and geese to tell 'em if sumthin's up. And they daren't take their guns to anyone now. Not that I'd be wantin' them to do that, mind."

"So what's the feeling in the pub?" asked Flaxby.

"Oh, you know how it is, sir. City lowlife. Boro, Sunderland... Newcastle maybe."

"You think so too?"

"Maybe. I'd like to know a bit more first," said Angells with his characteristic caution when faced with a lack of evidence. "It just doesn't sound like opportunists to me. It's not exactly the same as nippin' in and nippin' off with the family jewels while the owner's havin' a night out at the Metro, is it?"

He was referring to the Metro Centre—a large leisure complex on the outskirts of Gateshead. It was a lengthy drive from the becks on the Wear but there wasn't anywhere as large and as exciting that lay closer.

"You've got to know how to drive a tractor, and they don't exactly do the ton on the motorway, do they?" Angells added. "That's if they are driven away. From what I've heard, they just seem to vanish."

"OK, Mike," said Flaxby. "This farm thing has fallen into our lap. Don't want it—got a hundred other things to do—but there it is. The chief con and I went to a big meeting about these thefts yesterday, and she's come back full of ideas. Seems like you're one of 'em. She wants to see you, so... off you go upstairs."

"Now?"

"Right now."

Angells rose, but as he went to open the door, Flaxby called him back.

"Look, son," he said. "One more thing. Luke Babcock's out this week. I'm not expecting any problem—talk is easy, action's a hell of a lot harder—but, just in case, keep my personal number on your speed dial. One word—Babcock— and I'll get onto it and track you. OK?"

"OK, sir. No worries. Thank you."

"Oh, and you might as well take that pile of stuff with you, seeing as you offered!" Flaxby said lightly. "Computers seem to generate paperwork, not cut it down."

Angells smiled and returned for an armful of files before going out of the room and shutting the door behind him. He wasn't fooled by the super's parting levity though. First he checked he had Flaxby's number on his phone, and then he went to the chief constable's office.

* * *

Mike Angells, Raith's Angel Baby, was no sour, dour, angst-ridden misery! He'd got into all the normal childhood scrapes, spent the usual number of hours in A&E with a frantic mum as medics checked limbs damaged in climbs and tumbles, pubbed, clubbed and danced the night away, and had never had to come 'out', having never made much of an issue of being 'in'. He'd known he preferred Sam Mitford's company to that of any other kid in his class and when, mid-teens, he started to see that their mutual fondness went deeper than the need for a mate to kick a ball around with for an hour after tea, he accepted the realisation with the same good-humoured shrug of his shoulders as he accepted most other things. Most things—for, when he was eighteen years old, six months off his A levels, his father died and he got his first inkling of something Raith had known for years, that life wasn't always fair.

Bob Angells had worked in the stone industry, a quarryman loading the local 'marble' into trucks and sometimes driving the lorries himself. One November afternoon, after three days solid rain, the stretch of road he was driving over subsided, and he was buried under twelve tons of limestone.

With three younger sisters and a younger brother, an elderly grandparent living in the house as well, and bread to be put on the table....

"It doesn't brook no argument," Mike had told his mum. "There's still work over Kielder way. Not on the reservoir itself. They're buildin' this tunnel to transfer water through to Frosterley so that the towns on the Wear don't go short in the summer. I can get there on Dad's bike. I'm quittin' school."

And so, for the next two years, he developed his social skills and his muscles on a construction site, travelling the only way a car-less youngster in a bus-free world could: on two wheels, his two powered by a 600cc engine. Whenever he had a day off, he rode to Durham, to the hall of residence where Sam was living while he studied archaeology, and they'd spend their free hours exploring the hills and the coast and the country pubs before finding somewhere quiet and secluded where, for an hour or two, they lay closeted in each other's arms. No two ways about it: the two men were in love, and they were still in love, four years later, when Sam died too.

Waiting for Mike to bring the bike round in the car park of Emelda's, a gay nightclub close to the Metro Centre. Ploughed into by the drunk driver of a Merc, and dead on arrival at the hospital three-quarters of an hour later. So Sam had been buried in the little churchyard in the village where he had been christened twenty-five years earlier, and Mike applied himself to work with a single-mindedness that left as little room as possible for thinking about loss and what might have been. Fortunately, the job he was in by then didn't leave much time over for thinking.

The Kielder Project over, he'd joined the police and done his two-year probation. He'd proved his competence, completed a stint of 'ordinary' police work and then moved to the RPU, the Road Policing Unit, patrolling the busy north-east section of the M1/A1 on a big, hefty looking BMW R1200, twice the size of his own crimson Yamaha. But when government cutbacks affected policing, as well as other local public services, the RPU was scaled down and, thinking ahead, Mike had applied to CID, been interviewed, been accepted and found he had the money to go where he wanted. The problem was that the person he wanted to go where he wanted with was lying in Tunhead graveyard.

Chapter 2

Angells took the station stairs three at a time and, as Flaxby had directed, went straight to the chief constable's office.

"Come in and sit down, Mike," said the CC when Angells knocked, poked his head round her door and proffered a "Ma'am?"

Oh aye, cosy is it? he thought, alerted by the invitation to sit, as well as by the use of his first name. Chief Constable Mayfield was a stickler for protocol, and she dished out helpings of familiarity sparingly. And Angells was right to be watchful.

"I don't like it, ma'am," he said after she had outlined the plan.

In a nutshell, she wanted the Tun Beck farmers to be privy to and part of an operation that would catch the thieves red-handed.

"I appreciate you've no wish to mix your personal life in Tunhead with—"

"No, ma'am," he interrupted. "That too, but it isn't only that that's botherin' me."

"What then?"

"I just don't like involvin' civilians in police business, ma'am. There's always a danger that folk get hurt. Different if we get hurt. Risk of the job."

"I can't agree with you more, Mike, but so far, these thefts haven't involved any violence. I know," she added quickly, seeing his raised eyebrows, "everything's gone off so quietly that there hasn't been any need for violence, and you're right, there's always a first time. But look at the map, Mike. You can see where trouble's heading."

Angells had been looking.

"I know, ma'am. Sticks out a mile. Movin' westward. Eventually they'll come to us."

And Lynne Mayfield picked up on the inspector's 'us' and played a trump card straight away.

"If your Tun Beck farmers are anything like the farmers over in Yorkshire, where they've been having similar problems, they won't just stand there and do nothing if they see their tractors being stolen. They'll get involved with or without our support. Then they could really get hurt."

With great misgivings, Angells agreed.

"OK, Inspector…"

Angells stifled a smile. Cosy time over.

"I want you to go to Dansett Cross and liaise with a uniformed sergeant there. His name's Beckover. Do you know him?"

"No, ma'am. I thought I knew all the officers over that way."

"He's only been with us since a week last Friday. He's stepped in for Sergeant Jackson. She's still convalescing after that fall she took."

"Oh. OK. I went to visit her the other week. She told me that we're havin' to draft in a sergeant from another division, us being so short staffed."

"Tell me about it," moaned the CC. "The thing is, Beckover spent three years with the North Sea Harbour Police Unit, as the HPU was called at the time. He knows everything there is to know about the ports we think the thieves are shipping from, and you, better than any of us, know how things work at the farming end. I know it's not CID's usual menu, but under the circumstances, I want you involved. What about calling a meeting with some of the farmers?"

"I need to give it some thought, ma'am. There are no secrets in the Tunhope Arms. The whole of the North East would know about the op if we called a meetin', and that would include the gang doin' the liftin', assumin' it is a North East outfit."

He was silent for a minute, thinking. What was his caseload at the moment? Too large, for a start, including three rapes, one of which was incestuous, and a spate of what the sole perpetrator they'd caught so far had described as 'spaz-bashing'—a euphemism for some brutal attacks which had left one young wheelchair-bound boy too scared to leave the house and had terrified three others. If Angells had had illusions about the basic goodness of mankind, he'd lost them years ago—almost, for every time he crossed the broad stone bridge that spanned the Wear, and turned his back on the station and his face towards home, he felt his spirits rising. Not that he could describe his life in Tunhead as calm and peaceful, not with the constant to-ings and fro-ings of his rather unusual neighbours there, but he knew that all he had to do to shed work's burdens was sit in the churchyard or stroll up the track alongside the beck and out onto the moors. And if he wanted company, and not the solitude offered by curlew cries, heather and bones, then there was Ross, who, it seemed to him, instinctively read his mood and provided the comforts he required. Until, of course, Raith, seeing that their light was on, would come bounding across the garden like an oversized dog demanding mating rights. But he couldn't take umbrage with Raith.

His train of thought was interrupted.

"Inspector? Inspector!"

"Ma'am! Sorry. Just thinkin'."

What about? she wondered, given the little smile that had replaced the serious set of his lips.

"Do I have your permission to discuss this with my partner, ma'am? I ask because it might be possible to involve some of the other folk who live in Tunhead—the art crowd—and that's his line. Just with the surveillance. Give the farmin' families a rest. They work long enough hours as it is."

"Yes. Fine. In fact, that's not a bad idea. As long as you go to Dansett Cross tomorrow. Beckover is expecting you at ten."

* * *

Sergeant Beckover had, naturally, done some checking on the CID officer he'd been told he was working with, but as the best mouth to hear things from is always the horse's, he asked Sergeant Jackson directly as well.

"In a single sentence?" the invalid said, with her broken leg raised upon a stool. "Impossible. Can't do. Angells... Let's see... Not been an inspector long. Hard, but not cement yet. Shrewd, respected, well thought of... Wasn't he at this meeting then?"

"No. Just the CC and this Superintendent Flaxby."

"Mmm. Well, the super's a good man, but if he ever thought that one of his boys and girls was taking a bribe or doing anything to bring his beloved division into disrepute, he'd skin 'em alive. But beware. Angells is Flaxby's blue-eyed boy. Can't put a size ten wrong."

"Better be careful how I handle him then," said Beckover.

Sergeant Jackson smiled. "Not too closely, I suggest."

Next morning at 10 am, therefore, Sergeant Beckover was looking out of one of the station windows, waiting for the appearance of the man he mustn't handle closely. To his annoyance, a leather-clad biker roared into the little car park, chained his bike to a lamppost and casually sauntered out of sight.

Beckover went to the front desk.

"Some bloody biker's using us as his private car park, Tom," he began saying when, to the amusement of the long-serving duty PC, the biker came through the door, said, "Mornin', Tom!" and held out a hand in greeting to the astonished sergeant.

By the time they had eaten half a pack of biscuits, washed down by cups of strong station coffee, Beckover and Angells had formed the beginnings of a good working relationship. Few pleasantries. Straight to the matter at hand. Bearing in mind Jackson's warning, Beckover was polite and diplomatic.

"You know the Weardale area far better than I do, obviously, sir," he said, "so how do you see this working out?"

Angells looked him straight in the eye and said, "Depends how much freedom to act you reckon you have, and how far you're willin' to stretch what you've got."

Beckover hoped that he didn't look too puzzled.

"The way it was put to me," Angells continued, "we ask the farmers to leave stuff out or unlocked, and arrange for a nightly rota to act as a watch and raise the alarm. Mixture of farmers and cops, seein' as we're so short-staffed. Then the cavalry comes in and nabs the thieves."

Beckover nodded. That was the plan that had been discussed and decided on at Sunday's meeting.

"The chief said I could talk it through with my partner, and we both agreed—it won't work like that. Every farmer we know would be so bloody furious they'd stop at nuthin' to protect their property, and they'd want to belt the hell out of anyone who tried to steal it. More than that—they all have guns. They all know the law against usin' guns, but they'd want to use 'em. In the heat of a big fight, they just might. So instead of collarin' a gang of thieves, we'd end up collarin' the people we're tryin' to help."

He didn't add that, if a full-blooded fight broke out and he was there, he'd happily put himself into the thick of it. And happily break a few bones. He knew that more than the protection of property was at stake. This was about protecting a way of life, and there weren't too many parts of the country left where such a life could be protected.

"So did she come up with a better idea?"

"She?"

"Your partner."

Beckover had made an assumption about lifestyle arrangements but, thought Angells, not entirely an unexpected one.

"Would it make a difference to you workin' alongside me if the she were a he?" Angells said impassively.

There was nothing in his voice nor his face to suggest that this was a loaded question.

Beckover looked at him, suddenly realised why Jackson had told him to watch how he handled his visitor, shook his head and, laughing, said, "Of course it wouldn't. Why should it, sir?"

Why indeed? thought Angells. Well, it would to at least one person he could mention.

"I think," he said carefully, "that it would be more sensible, and more profitable, to collar the gang as far away from the Tun Beck farms as possible. At the port itself, in fact. That way, the farmers don't get hurt. We discover how the stuff's gettin' out of the country, and we break up the shippin' arrangements. OK, it might all start up again, but much more slowly than if we just nicked the gang red-handed; and maybe by the time it's all up and runnin' again, we'd have this dedicated task force in place that the chief was tellin' me about. Like they have in Yorkshire."

Angells waited.

"That's way beyond the brief, sir," said Beckover, concerned that throwing out the plan agreed at the meeting might not be the quickest way to gain the accolades and promotion he felt that his track record deserved. On the other hand, Angells was the superior officer. He'd be the one to take the stick if this all went bottoms up.

"Yes. It is," agreed Angells. "But what's the point of just nickin' the shiters at this end? Chances are that, even if they squeal, they only know their own part in the gang. Ops are interrupted, but only till new drivers are found. All starts up again fast. Seems to me we have to look at the port end. And this way, the farmers don't get hurt, because they know they have to stay quiet and let the thieves get away."

"That's true. So you're thinking what? That we'd fit trackers to everything that moves?"

"State-of-the-art GPS is what I'd like, but I doubt there's the cash to cover everything. Thing is, my partner and I were lookin' last night. We don't think the farms higher up the valley, Tunhead way, are in the greatest danger—yet, that is. Have you had a chance to look round?"

"No, sir, and that end of the Wear's a foreign country to me."

"Well, the road gets very narrow higher up the Tun valley, and there's no way out 'cept back the way you come," Angells explained. "Very few passin' places. Can't see a big artic manoeuverin' too easily. Everyone would be out with brushes for swords and easels for shields if they drove up in the middle of the night and tried to turn."

"Sir? Brushes? Easels?"

"Tunhead's an artists' enclave," Angells explained, smiling. "An *artisan's* enclave, I should say. I'm the only normal person there!"

"Oh, I see," Beckover said, smiling himself whilst wondering what might pass for art in an off-the-beaten-track sort of spot like Tunhead. Quickly dismissing some possibilities, he said, "Furniture van?"

"Not if we're lookin' at containers."

"Mmm. Agreed."

"There are three farms lower down the valley closer to the A road. See? On your map there?"

Angells went to the wall where a map was hanging a little lopsidedly. He straightened it up and pointed.

"These three farms. We think they're more likely targets. All the other farms would come in and help do a rota, though. No doubt about that. Everyone would pull together. Problem would be stoppin' everyone else in the county knowin'."

Beckover nodded. Angells was clearly right about the transport logistics.

"The thing is," the inspector continued, "which port? Sergeant?"

Over to me, thought Beckover.

"My feeling's Hartlepool," he said firmly. "Not Tyneside. Too far. Could be Sunderland, but I doubt it. There'd be too many speed cams and police patrols on the Durham–Sunderland stretch. There's Boro, but it's such a big, controlled operation there. I think they'd go for somewhere smaller where they could keep an eye on things."

Angells was looking at the map again. "They wouldn't even have to leave the 689," he said. "Straight to the port and off to China or somewhere. I don't know the set-up at Hartlepool. Is there enough warehousin' and storage?"

"Plenty."

"Do you still have contacts there? I understand you were with the HPU."

"Plenty of contacts, too, sir."

"Then we go with your feelin', Sergeant, and maybe between the two of us we can stop these thefts and let the farmers get on with their farmin'."

* * *

For a long time after Sam Mitford's death, Mike had found it hard, very hard, to let go of the past and, uninterested in forming any new serious relationship, he seemed married to his job. So, it was a slightly bewildered Angells who had driven home from work one evening and, picking at the topping on a pizza, had chewed over the day's events.

He'd been a sergeant at the time, and he'd been sent to an art gallery in Durham. Some expensive exhibition pieces had gone missing. After a useful talk with the show curator, a man around his own age with smiling eyes, a nice light voice and a very un-arty-farty manner, he'd agreed to return the following day with some ideas on security, now that he knew something of the set-up.

Next morning, to his surprise and embarrassment, he found himself choosing what to wear with a care that would have been more suited to a night's clubbing than to a day's work, but the curator had been dressed so 'becomingly' (that was the word that had entered Mike's mind) that he felt the need to make a good impression. In fact, he needn't have bothered to try, and he could have turned up in a grass skirt with flowers round his neck if he'd had a mind to do so.

The curator had already taken in all he needed to with a glance of his artistic eye, and Angells' second appearance simply confirmed the impression he'd gained at the first. The curator wanted this man. Wanted him to sit for a painting, model for a sculpture, pose for a photograph. *Be honest*, he'd told himself. Wanted to fuck him and be fucked by him. Wanted to be kissed and enveloped in his strong arms. *Oh dear,* he realised, *You have got it bad!* These, somewhat amended, were the very words the object of the curator's desire was telling *him*self as he drove to the gallery to meet his admirer.

And Mike Angells, who could, with confidence, ask rapists and serial killers the most searching questions, sat behind the wheel of a Ford Fiesta and couldn't for the life of him decide on a chat-up line for a law-abiding gallery curator named Ross Whitburn-Howe.

Fortunately, Ross had been considering the same question, but more effectively.

"If you have time, Sergeant," he'd said with a broad smile, "I can give you a personal showing."

It crossed Angells' startled mind that the curator was offering to strip naked. *Stop it! Wishful thinking,* he told himself, but he could see by the laughter in Whitburn's eyes that his momentary look of astonishment had been interpreted correctly.

"I can spare ten minutes," he said, as formally as he could, given that he had some confusion as to whether the personal showing would be for work or pleasure.

The curator looked at him, and again, Angells felt that his mind was being dissected as easily as a scalpel sliced the flesh of a cadaver in the morgue.

Oh dear, thought Ross. *He's bothered now. Wants to, but beset by uncertainty. Why? I wonder. So, do I tread carefully, or do I risk it? What can go wrong? Well, for a start, he could turn on his heels and pretend he's got to go and solve a murder. But, nothing ventured, and other less memorable clichés.*

"This way," he instructed brightly, and led Angells straight to a sculpture created by Raith Balan.

"This is one of our major exhibits," he explained, scrutinising Angells' face as carefully as Angells himself might have scrutinised a suspect's in the interview room.

Angells allowed his gaze to roam over a construction that, to his unpractised eye, resembled intertwined strings of Cumberland sausage. He wasn't surprised that this one hadn't been stolen. Who in God's name would want it? Looking more carefully, though, he could see that it had two heads, four arms and four legs, but the limbs were fused together in such a way that there only seemed to be one body.

Ross watched expectantly. Angells looked at him.

"Any reason why you've brought me to this

piece rather than all those others?" he asked. His eyes were smiling, even though his tone was inquisitorial.

Jump in! For goodness sake, jump in! He can only walk out. You'll be no worse off than before, Ross thought. Aloud, he said, "I thought you might like to reconstruct the scene of the crime. Not that there's been one, of course." He waited.

"Not since '67 anyway. Mind you, public place. 2000. Could be minors present."

The curator smiled. He knew the law too *and* which Acts of Parliament Angells was referring to.

"Sergeant Angells?"

"Yes?"

"Do you have a name? I mean, you know mine's Ross."

"Mike."

"Mike? Then, Mike, would you like to have dinner with me this evening?"

And tomorrow evening and the next evening and the next and into eternity and beyond.

"I'd like that very much."

And so began the happiest time of Mike Angells' life.

* * *

Phil

There are easier tasks than making a polyamorous lifestyle work. It works for us because we work at it. For most lovers, compromise means seeing things from two sides. We have to see things from four, and the only way to do that without falling out over what, from a cosmic viewpoint, are mere dust-sized particles is to talk. And talk. And talk. We do an enormous amount of talking and negotiating. Raith tends to become animated: he wears his heart on his paint-covered sleeves, but that's fine because it draws problems out into the open. Ross is skilled at smoothing things over. He's used to dealing diplomatically with awkward people—not that I would call any of us awkward. Mike, verbally, is always the least involved. He'd rather listen, but then he'll say something really pithy or ask a pertinent question. I imagine it's akin to handling an interview at the station. And whatever is decided at these sessions, we ensure that we do.

Most talk happens, naturally, in Cromarty. That's the name we bestowed on Mike and Ross's house. The four of us rarely meet at mine (too far), and we enter Raith's only under duress. His studio doubles as his living accommodation, and unless Mike can provide us with a steady supply of disposable forensics overalls to go with my oxygen masks, we're staying out of it for fear of choking to death on clay dust.

We're really serious about the need to sit down together, and it isn't always easy. We all work irregular hours, and both Mike and I can get called away in the middle of our discussions. So, if one in the morning is the only time to sit at the negotiating table, then one in the morning it is. We never let anything build to crisis level. We always flatten our molehills before they rise to mountains. Not always easy, but we manage.

Chapter 3

Six weeks after their initial meeting in Dansett Cross, Inspector Angells and Sergeant Beckover met again, this time in Warbridge to reciprocate thanks for a job well done. They had just delivered their final report to CC Mayfield and Chief Superintendent Crane, Beckover's head of Uniformed Branch, and been cynically amused to note how, in the light of the op's success, their loose interpretation of the brief had not even been referred to.

Angells graciously stressed the importance of Beckover's local knowledge and generously played down his own part in securing the excellent result. The very tiny piece of him that did enjoy appreciation received it from the only source he ever wished to.

"Well done, lad," said Flaxby. "Grand job. Worth a month's free drinking in that pub of yours, I should have thought."

That was praise a-plenty and should have been the icing on the cake. Not that Angells craved praise, and not that he ever expected any. He'd do his job well because doing so gave him self-respect. The way he looked at things, the respect of others was good to have and pleasing, but he had to look at himself in the mirror every morning, not them.

To his surprise, on this occasion, his super's

appreciation discomforted him. Mike knew full well his reasons for encouraging the escalation of the brief. Much to do with maximising the disruption to the gang who were behind the thefts, and much to do with the farmers' safety, but he'd also had a desire to prevent the world 'out there' from encroaching upon the little haven he had come to cherish.

The instant the chief had outlined her plan, he'd felt uneasy but, at the time, he could hardly have halted the conversation to analyse the reasons. His day was then so busy, spent doing his own work as well as tidying up the super's, that it wasn't until he was travelling home that evening that he'd found the time to think. He'd known Ross would be late, too late to share a meal together, and he hadn't fancied one of Raith's 'stick it all in the pan along with a teaspoon of chilli flakes' experiments, so he'd pulled into a layby where he knew there'd be a burger van and the chance of a good strong cup of tea. Eating and drinking, he gave vent to his musings, interspersing them with observations about the other travellers. A brake light missing, a noisy exhaust, driving away without seat belts. It was hard to stop being a cop. *It probably isn't easy being the partner of a cop either*, he'd thought and, in acknowledgement of that admission, he'd turned his thoughts specifically to Ross.

If his lot chased the thieves higher up the valley, into Tunhead, they'd be like cornered cats. Then what would they do? Fight their way out? Grab a hostage and barter? They could grab Ross. He could be hurt. The idea had filled Mike with horror. Who else did he know who was generous enough, kind enough, understanding enough to share him with a doctor, a sculptor and a box of bones? The answer was obvious. No one. Phil had no problem about sharing and no problem with the bones per se, but he'd never move to Tunhead and Mike would never leave, so Phil could never be a substitute for Ross. Raith? The problem with Raith was Raith himself. Generous to a fault, and kind and loving, and oh-so-sexy, but about as stable as a ticking bomb. Not Raith, then.

He asked a lot of Ross, he realised, and Ross had never ever let him down.

* * *

Ross

A winter's tale:

For four years I was the only other person in Mike's life. Then one winter's evening, he was more subdued than usual. He didn't ask his normal questions about the show I'd just put on: Who came? What sold? And so on. Not that he's really interested, but he's good at pretending that he is. No, that's doing Mike an injustice. He's interested in *me*, so he's interested in what I do. This time, though, he didn't ask.

I said, "What's the matter, love? Is it a case?" That was the obvious thing. Sometimes, his work would weigh on his mind, especially in winter when it was dark and cold and icy and there was no scenery visible on the journey home to raise the spirits. He had to keep both eyes glued to the stretch of road in his headlights, and he'd tumble through the door, knackered with the effort.

"Not a case, no," he answered.

I love the way he says "no" —comes out as "nor". I tease him sometimes just to make him say it.

He's just finished his dinner, a big one:

"Do you want some more?"

"Nor ta. Aa'm stuffed t' burstin'!"

We've just had sex:

"Do you want it again?"

"Nor ta. Y' mus' be jorkin'!"

So I'd waited, half knowing what the matter was, because this happened after the fifth or sixth time he'd stayed overnight at Phil's.

When he first told me that he wanted Phil as a lover as well as me, I was really hurt. It wasn't a being-dumped sort of hurt. It was more that I felt I was being told I was inadequate, insufficient for his needs, and I was bewildered too. Was I doing something wrong? Or doing too much? Or too little?

I'm no prude. The instant I met Mike I knew I wanted him—near me, under me, over me, inside me… all the locative prepositions you can think of-me, and I made sure I got him, and we spent some wonderful (monogamous) years in the little house he'd bought to be near Sam. (That didn't bother me, by the way. I'll explain later.) So, when he told me about Phil…

Do you know, I hadn't had any idea that what I'd been offering Mike wasn't enough? Out of bed we enjoyed each other's company. Enough in common to do things together. Enough differences to preserve plenty of individuality. Plenty to chat about if we felt like it. Easy silences if we didn't. We both kept irregular hours. It made our time together more precious and we understood that, sometimes, dinner would be late or burnt or cold or non-existent. Par for a detective's and an arts curator's course. And in bed, we switched roles. I never had reason to say, "I've got a headache," and I was always ready and willing, but—well—it clearly wasn't enough.

At first, I was scared I'd lose him completely. It took a heck of a lot of talking and reassurance to make me see I wouldn't, that he wasn't looking for a substitute. I'm not even sure he knew what he was looking for. There are ways in which he's very needy. I think this was simply one of the ways, and I'm willing to make allowances. He's worth it, as the adverts say of hair.

So my lover was unfaithful but, eventually, we sorted it. Phil wasn't an invading army, for a start. He didn't try to take over the house. In fact, he rarely came here. Whatever occurred between him and Mike occurred between them in Warbridge, not Tunhead. That changed. Phil comes here now and, sometimes, we're three in the bed, but now I don't feel threatened by his presence. He's always been respectful of the fact that I've first claim on the property, if that makes sense. Phil's OK. He's a good man. There's a sense in which I love him very much, and I trust him completely.

I remember saying that if ever Mike needed patching up, at least I knew a man who could. The things you say in jest, heh?

Chapter 4

Besides the obvious benefits to the local farming community, two positives arose from the Tun Beck farm op that had great importance for Angells personally, though he had no idea how important they would turn out to be.

Firstly, he gained a grateful colleague. Leg mended, Sergeant Jackson was back on duty, and Beckover returned to his own division. He soon found himself promoted to inspector, partly due, as he knew, to the praise heaped onto him by Mike.

Secondly, one of the gang involved at the Hartlepool end of things squealed and furnished evidence of other similar crimes, and these Angells was particularly interested in. As more and more sealed containers bound for the Far East and Africa were opened up, items stolen from various building and construction sites saw the light of day again. Angells was able to retrieve thousands of pounds worth of equipment and return it to grateful owners on his patch.

Favours were owed, and when Angells' life took an unexpected and unwanted turn a few months later, he called the favours in.

There was at least one negative result, however. Angells' confused feelings had not passed unnoticed at the station.

"What's up with the inspector?" Fortune enquired of Superintendent Flaxby some days after the completion of the op.

Flaxby pulled a face. He'd noticed something too.

"Up in what way?" he asked noncommittally.

"Seems to have lost his sparkle."

"So would you if you'd been on that farm rota night after night for weeks," said Flaxby.

"Maybe. Or maybe it's those three men of his keeping him from his beauty sleep."

You can't resist it, can you? thought Flaxby.

He pretended to ignore the remark, but when he returned to his office, he sat down, worried. So Fortune knew about the others, did he? Angells made no secret of the fact that his partner was another man. Indeed, Ross had come to various social events with him, although the two men hadn't, as yet, partnered each other for the final waltz of the night. Ross had tales to tell about household names in the art and chat-show worlds, which made him a welcome addition to any cocktail party or sit-down dinner. What's more, he was lively, funny, intelligent, un-pompously cultured and clearly enamoured of his police escort. Everyone knew about Angells and Ross, but not so many people knew of the other men in Angells' life.

Flaxby had learnt of the polyamorous relationship some two years previously when he had discussed with Angells, then a sergeant, his promotion to inspector. Maintaining the public's trust in the Force was difficult at the best of times, and Flaxby could imagine the fun the local press would have suggesting that Warbridge's safety lay in the hands of an adulterous, promiscuous, gay senior officer.

"You wear a wedding ring," Flaxby had said,

"but the two of you didn't marry, did you?"

"Officially, no, sir," said Angells. "Ours is a civil partnership. Not a same-sex marriage."

"Are you likely to marry?"

Angells looked surprised. He wasn't sure where this line of questioning was heading. "Sir?"

"Well?"

"I doubt it, sir. This seems more equal somehow. A partnership. Why do you ask?"

"Because if you're not married, you can't commit adultery, can you? And if you can't commit adultery, the *Echo* can't splash a headline about a gay, adulterous cop over its front page, can it? I know that, strictly speaking, adultery doesn't apply to same-sex marriage, but that wouldn't stop the *Echo* from sticking its awl in and doing its bit of damage. I doubt if they could spell 'polyamorist', though, let alone know what it means."

"Not sure *I* do, sir. I've not really thought of it as havin' a name. It's just what I do, and I'm just me."

"Well, whatever you are and whatever it is, is it meant to be a secret?"

"No, sir. Of course not. I've never been secretive about my life. You know that. I don't broadcast the poly thing around but that's partly because of Phil—I mean, he works in the hospital here—and partly to give Ross a break. There are all sorts of different lifestyles in Ross's world, and people aren't fazed by the one we have, but they can be curious, and he doesn't always want the questions—especially as, in one sense, he, personally, isn't polyamorous. Though, in another sense, he is."

"Oh," said Flaxby, "I assumed... You mean... I can see what you mean. I apologise."

"No need. It's fine."

"Perhaps he should get your Raith Balan to

make some little information leaflets, and he could hand them out to all these nosey people."

"Curious rather than nosey, I think, but no. Ross is far too savvy to hand out Raith's stuff like it was flyers for a rave or sumthin'. He'd sell 'em, mind!" He laughed, all the sparkle there. "So it's no secret, but I don't think that many people in the station know."

Which is why Superintendent Flaxby was surprised at his chief inspector's remark. Concerned, too. Perhaps the DCI was right. Perhaps there was something going on in Tunhead that was causing sleepless nights. Perhaps having three lovers *was* taking its toll.

Shite! That's the kind of thing Fortune would say, Flaxby thought with shame. But shame didn't stop him worrying.

At the same time as their superiors were heaping praise on Angells' and Beckover's shoulders, two uniformed constables, Rogers and Jacobs, were attending to an incident outside a gay bar in Warbridge town centre. This was, after all, an area of England where gay men stood more chance of hooking up with a Martian on Grindr than with another gay, and where separate clubs and bars remained the safest place for socialising.

This particular morning, a man was shouting obscenities at the bar's customers from the pavement outside. It had happened before and, previously, the staff had dealt with the loudmouth themselves rather than involve that symbol of all they deemed wrong with the Establishment—the local police. This time, though, the man, who was blind drunk, was occasionally following people in. Fed up with his ranting and concerned that events would escalate, the head barman had phoned the station, and the two PCs had driven quickly round.

They recognised the ranter immediately and hauled him off to quieten down and sober up. Niall Tomlinson by name, he was a sad case really— rarely sober, and always abusive when drunk. The abuse could be directed at anything and anyone. He was, depending on what was in his head at any particular time, xenophobic, islamophobic, gynophobic and, on the day in question, homophobic. For his own safety, as well as for the safety of the men and women he shouted at and cursed, he sometimes needed to cool off in a prison cell. Rogers and Jacobs, knowing that he had, on occasions, turned violent, had taken hold of him firmly and driven him back to the station, where he could sleep and wake with nothing more than a bad hangover.

This little incident had repercussions for Inspector Angells too.

* * *

Ross

Sometimes, people say to me, "Oh, you're in a polyamorous relationship, are you?" (or words to that effect, as 'polyamorous' doesn't slide too smoothly into most casual conversation) and I say, "Mike is. I'm not. I'm in a purely monogamous one." Then they look puzzled, or else incredulous, as it's obvious we're a quad.

Well, firstly, we don't cohabit. There are three addresses on the census forms. Mike and I live together in one of the old quarrymen's houses in Tunhead. It's a tiny hamlet at the head of Tun Beck. The houses were built to house quarrymen and their families. Raith lives in Tunhead too, across the street in a converted storehouse—the ground floor is his studio—and Phil lives twenty miles away in Warbridge, near where he works at the hospital. So we officially live separately, even though, most of the time, at least one property has empty beds and, often, everyone seems to squash in here. I don't mean in bed! We'd be packed tighter than tinned sardines if we tried that. I just mean in the house. It's only tiny, though we've extended the kitchen as much as we could: Tun Beck runs through the back garden. But I'm getting away from the point—my "am I/aren't I poly" status.

Secondly, I only fuck with Mike, though he fucks with both of them, and they fuck with each other. Does that make me polyamorous? I'm not sure, but I think not.

The other three are shaking their heads and grinning. Bastards.

Chapter 5

Mike didn't usually use his bike to travel from Tunhead to the station, but at least once a week he'd visit his brother's house in Crook to see how things were doing. The brother in question worked away from home, surrounded by water on a North Sea oil rig. Angells never went empty handed, but he knew that what his two young nephews really wanted was to take turns at riding pillion, and he was happy to oblige. So, first one and then the other would don a helmet and some little leathers, and off they'd go to a roar of revs that made them think they were doing a ton up the M1, but Angells would quickly kill the speed and ride around sedately for five minutes. No matter, they loved it.

So, this particular day, he rode his bike to work. As it was the school summer holidays, and he was on lates, he'd ridden to Crook in the morning, and he arrived for work at quarter to two.

"Angela!" called DCI Fortune as the inspector passed his door. "In here, if you will."

Will not! thought Angells, but knowing he hadn't really been offered a choice, he went in and asked, "What, Ron?"

"You know Manny's Bar?" Fortune asked in a tone that suggested that the question was rhetorical: he didn't wait for an answer. "I'm stuck here, so get over there, will you? Else we'll have some Tynesider from Major Crimes coming down and telling us what to do. One of the Docs and a couple of uniformed are waiting. Looks suspicious. Death in the gents."

He made the recent fatality sound like an allusion to a recently unearthed Agatha Christie novel.

Angells nodded his acquiescence. "It's a gay bar," he said dispassionately.

"Well, fancy that! Should be right up your street then," said the DCI provocatively.

"I just meant that, chances are, there won't be many witnesses waiting around, and probably none that'd want to talk to us," Angells explained calmly.

"Well switch on the charm and you might even get yourself a date with one of them, but if you don't get your arse back on your bike pretty quickly, you'll miss your opportunity."

"Yes, sir," said Angells as he re-zipped his jacket.

He was practised in creating some uncertainty. Was the 'sir' sarcastic or respectful? Damn it. Fortune didn't know.

* * *

Angells stopped at the traffic lights that lay close to Police HQ. Had he been riding home, he would have sidled up to the car closest to the lights and got ready to accelerate quickly away, but he wasn't, so he waited, engine idling in mid-lane, fourth in a line of traffic, and allowed himself the luxury—or curse—of contemplation.

He mused about the wisdom of sending the station's sole gay cop to investigate a suspicious death in a gay bar.

He wasn't the only person Fortune could have sent to Manny's. Did the chief inspector actually think that Angells would genuinely be the best one on the case? Perhaps he believed that Angells being gay would result in some sort of heightened empathy towards the witnesses—'gaympathy', if there was such a word.

No, it couldn't be that. Neither Fortune nor Angells himself had much truck with the notion that being gay somehow meant that you automatically had a higher-than-average sensitivity reading. Some gays did and some gays didn't. It happened that, as he knew, he was one of the ones who did, but he didn't attribute it to his being gay, as such.

No, he decided, this was all just another barb pulled from Fortune's quiver and fired in his direction. Nothing so much fun as causing Angells embarrassment.

As Angells saw it, the problem wasn't how much, as a gay man, *he* would be expected to perceive, but rather how he would *be* perceived. Although relations had vastly improved, history was hard to forget, and the one thing that Warbridge's gay men still loathed above all others was what they felt was the bigoted, prejudiced police force. Would gay witnesses see him solely as a detestable cop or, in the event that they sussed him out, as a traitor to the cause?

"Can't win either way," Angells said to himself.

So he felt he'd be in for a painfully rough ride, assuming anyone had stuck around Manny's Bar to be ridden.

A driver honked from the car behind, steered round him and through an open window shouted, "You stuck fast, mate? That what the "fast" in "Fast and Flying" means?"

Fast and Flying was stencilled onto the back

of Angells' bike leathers. It was both a reference to his fondness for road speed and a play on his name.

He resisted the temptation to return the driver's two-finger greeting with one of his own. Receiving rude gestures was par for the course for a black-leathered biker and, anyway, you never knew how folk would react if you gave them a two-fingers back. *CID Inspector In Road Rage Punch Up.* He could imagine what Flaxby would say if he saw that on the front page of the *Echo*! And what Flaxby would do! There were a lot of things the super would put up with, but bringing his precious division into disrepute wasn't one of them. Angells would feel more than just verbal punches if that happened. So, Angells once again ignored a provocation and rode, fairly calmly, on to Manny's Bar.

It only took five more minutes to reach his destination. He left his bike between a marked police car and a car he recognised as belonging to Dr Dorling, the on-duty police medic. Dorling could be relied upon to provide an accurate initial assessment of cause of death, so Angells felt his spirits rise a little.

Forensics were there already, taking prints and photographs and crawling like large white mice all over the floor. Angells introduced himself to the bar staff and then walked over to the doctor and to the uniformed constable who had been first on the scene and was impatiently waiting beside him.

The doctor and the inspector exchanged nods of recognition.

"Fill me in, then go if you like, Doc," said Angells.

When Angells was properly suited up, the doctor pointed to the body. A man lay on his side on the toilet floor with a small puddle of blood near his head. Even in his death, one could see he'd once been full of life: tanned, strong and young, possibly mid-twenties. Angells crouched down beside him.

"Could he just have fallen, Doc? Drugs? Alcohol? Some kind of fit?" he asked, looking up at the doctor.

Doc Dorling shook his head. "Substances? I doubt it, though I can't say for certain until the toxicology report. No marks and no smell of drink on his breath. A fit? Wouldn't rule it out, but we'll know more after the post-mortem and got hold of his medical records. But I don't think so, given the way he fell. It looks as though he was standing at the sink then hit his head, twice. There's a gash on his temple" —the doctor bent down and raised the dead man's head so that Angells could see— "and there's a second one on the back of his head. I'd say he made contact with the corner of that condom dispenser there." He pointed. "Then lost balance, fell and hit his temple on the sink."

"Which begs the question, how did he make contact with the dispenser?" Angells said, more to himself than to the doctor. "Which would kill him? The dispenser or the sink?"

"First question: that's for you to find out. Next two: the sink, I'd say. Be like hitting concrete," the doctor added firmly.

"I see. Anything else at this stage?"

The doctor shook his head. "No," he said, "other than I'd say he died instantly."

"Then thank you, Doc," said Angells. "What do we know about him?" he asked, turning to the uniformed constable. "PC Bartlett, isn't it? From South Shields."

By God, he's quick, thought the constable

with surprise as he confirmed that Angells had his details correct. He'd only been seconded to Warbridge a week before.

"ID?"

"Yes, sir. His name's John Coverham. Twenty-six. Lives in Bishop. On his driving licence."

"Anybody gone there? Next of kin?"

"Not yet, sir. We thought we'd better wait for you guys." He hastily added the word "sir" as he saw Angells' look. Perhaps 'you guys' had been too familiar a way of referring to CID. From a uniformed newcomer, anyway.

"Anything else? Mobile? Job? Wallet?"

"No mobile, sir, and it wasn't robbery. His wallet's stuffed full. Cards and notes. His job, yes—he was a soccer player. Ormerley. League One. Not long promoted from League Two," added the constable confidently.

"Bloody hell," said Angells, aware that the death of a soccer player would triple the media interest—which would be heightened anyway because of the gay connection. "We'll get onto them. Did you manage to hold onto any witnesses?"

"Only the guy who found him, sir. He's still here with his mates."

"The footballer's mates?"

Are they daft round here? PC Bartlett wondered. *Who does he think I mean?* "No, sir," he said. "His own. Everyone else was off sharp."

That was no surprise to Angells.

"OK. Thank you," he said, to PC Bartlett's surprise. "Hang on till the doctor's finished, will you? And you, Doc, do you think we can get a definite cause of death quickly? I'm just thinking of the press…"

"Point taken. I'll go and arrange the PM."

"Thank you again," said Angells who, whilst

rarely expecting any thanks for his own part in an investigation—it was, after all, what he was paid to do—was always ready to say "thank you" to others. He'd sometimes wondered why. It was their job too.

"I mustn't be sexist, but you have inherently good man-management techniques," Ross had told him with a naughty twinkle in his eye when, once, they'd been discussing Angells' modus operandi, *"and moreover, you've a natural courtesy."* Both were true, though the courtesy could vanish in an instant when a crime, or a DC's incompetence, demanded it was left behind.

Angells spent a few minutes talking to the customer who'd discovered the body. Then, having sent him and his mates home, he went to the bar to talk to the head barman.

Without waiting to be asked, the barman, whose name—according to the pendant on his neck chain—was Will, poured two glasses of apple juice and offered one to Angells, who took it with another "thank you." He unzipped a pocket to pull out some money, but the barman said, "On the house," and pointed to a table and chairs. The two of them sat down.

"Is this the new uniform we've all been hearing about then?" asked Will, looking at Angells' Lewis Leathers appreciatively.

Angells returned the examining gaze steadily.

"I know my leathers," the barman continued, "and yours are Super Phantoms. Bit steep even on an inspector's pay, I'd have thought," he said.

"Can you think about the dead man in your lav instead?" said Angells drily, secretly pleased to have his costly made-to-measure jacket recognised and complimented by such an obviously knowledgeable person. He'd tell Ross when he got home; the leathers had been a birthday present. "Is he a regular?"

"No, not according to the rest of the staff, and I didn't recognise him either. Nor the guy he was with."

"This guy he was with… That customer I just sent off said he was with another guy, but he didn't take much notice of him except to note they were arguin'. Not to give us a good description, anyway. Slim, early twenties, brown hair and jeans. Can't do much with that. Can you come up with sumthin' better?" asked Angells.

He took his pen out of an inside pocket, ready to take some notes, but the barman wasn't about to be rushed, or fazed, by Angells' refusal to be side-tracked.

Angells was left handed, and it was that hand that had gone to his pocket. "Nice wedding ring, too, Inspector," he said, noting the broad gold band on Angells' third finger. "Look, Inspector," he explained good-naturedly, "I'd like to say that working in a gay bar six days a week gives me GESP—gay extrasensory perception—but I can't. Ted over there—" He pointed to one of the bar staff, who waved in their direction and smiled. "He told me. You're quite out about it, right? Though you don't come in here."

"Sussed," said Angells, acknowledging Ted's wave and realising that he might have to take this slowly. At least he'd been offered a drink. "The body… Or would you like to see the weddin' pictures first?" Hopefully not, as there weren't any.

The barman smiled. "I'm all yours," he said, and told the DI as much as he was able.

Angells spent the rest of his shift preparing for the meeting that would take place the next morning. By the time he'd collated all the reports, which the DCs were feeding him at a rate to cause indigestion in the strongest stomach, stuck pins onto boards to represent surveillance cameras and sightings of the man seen arguing with the victim, filled in the DCI and super, organised liaison with the football club, arranged contact with the next of kin and done the countless other tasks that were required, it was late to return to Tunhead, especially as he'd be expected to be at the station bright and early to provide an authoritative briefing. He'd have ridden to Phil's and spent the night there, but Phil was at Raith's, and Mike didn't fancy an empty house. Instead, he rode home to snatch a few hours' sleep.

He seemed to be back at work almost as soon as he'd left it.

"Take us through it, Inspector," said the super when, next morning, the chairs and desk edges in the incident room had been filled with personnel, and cups of tea and one of coffee had been brought to those who mattered.

Angells rose and stood beside one of the information boards he'd prepared the evening before. He summarised his knowledge with trademark clarity, revealing none of the turmoil in which he'd spent those too-few hours back in Tunhead.

The problem was his nightmares. Most nights, they'd wake him up, and until gentle words and even gentler caresses could calm him and soothe him, he'd struggle to return to any sleep, let alone a peaceful, restful one. The worst dream was always the same. Not his job, with flashbacks of the very dangerous situations it sometimes forced him into. He had those too, but he accepted them as simply something he had to live with. But this dream… a car park, a crashed Mercedes, a limp body and a feeling of utter helplessness. That's what woke him up. Phil and Raith were good about it, kind and understanding of the fact that grief took many forms and, in some cases, endured many years, but Ross was more than good. The number of times Ross had let his own sleep be destroyed to ensure that his partner could have some rest! Consoling, caressing, always patient. Mike felt lucky to have Phil and Raith. He felt blessed to have Ross.

"One: John Jake Coverham," he began, pointing to a photograph. "Single. Twenty-six. Currently livin' in Bishop. Born Northampton. Pro soccer player. Moved north four years ago on a contract with United. Didn't work out, in part because of injuries. Signed for Ormerley last season.

"Two: Found dead in the gents in Manny's Bar at one fifteen yesterday afternoon. Immediate cause of death, accordin' to the PM: struck left temple on the edge of this sink." He pointed to another photo. "Gash on the back of his head consistent with the notion that, first, he made contact with a dispenser on the wall—blood on the edge of it—lost his balance and fell.

"Three: Cause of fall. No marks to suggest he was pushed. No contusions other than those consistent with the fall described. No medical history of epilepsy, blackouts or similar. No drugs. No alcohol. Seems to've slipped on a puddle of water, but accident? Pushed? We're keepin' an open mind at this stage of the investigation." He paused to let this sink in.

"Four: Identified by his brother. He's stayin' at the Travelodge. Lives in Derby. Brother surprised when asked about the victim's sexuality. Far as he knew, the dead man was straight. Didn't recall girlfriends or boyfriends and, far as he knew, the victim had no enemies. Sally?"

"That's right, sir," said the DC thus addressed. She had dealt with the brother and had looked into that part of the investigation. "I got the impression that they weren't close. So maybe there was someone the brother didn't know about."

Angells nodded. "Looks like at least one person."

He pointed to an enlarged, enhanced photo taken from a street camera a couple of hundred metres from the bar.

A uniformed constable came into the room and, excusing himself, gave Superintendent Flaxby a message.

"Update me later, Inspector," Flaxby said, rising to leave. "Another matter's cropped up."

"Sir." Angells nodded, and continued once Flaxby had left. "Five: Suspects. One possible. We need to find this man. Seen arguin' with the dead man—quietly arguin', not in-your-face threats—for a good thirty minutes. Came into Manny's together. Some hand holdin'—not too welcomed by Coverham, more the other guy. This was clocked at one seventeen, so he'd left just before the body was found. Not seen leavin'. Could've left by the door on this back alley here." He pointed to a door on a diagram he'd sketched of the premises' layout. "Was a warm day and the staff'd left this door open. We've got him runnin' along Sefton Street and Ardley Street—here, here and here." Angells pointed to three of the coloured pins representing street cameras "Then there's a stretch without surveillance, and we lose him. Can't pick him up again. We're tryin' taxis, bus station and car parks—all the usual, naturally.

"Six: Witnesses. The head barman had never

seen either man before, and neither had the other staff and customers we spoke to. The barman's provided a list of regulars he recalls were there and we're followin' that up." He paused.

"Seven. Like the brother," he continued a little uneasily, "the Ormerley lot were dismissive of any gay connection. Accordin' to them, he was a straight, hardworkin' player—defender—with no enemies, et cetera, et cetera, but he *was* gay, or bi anyway. He'd had unprotected sex a few hours before he died and...."

"Why don't I spare your blushes, Inspector?" interrupted Fortune, who, up till that moment, had been sitting quietly by. "What our inspector's trying manfully to say is that the lad had done it up the bum and—am I right about the terminology, Inspector, you having first-hand experience of these things? He'd topped? Traces of shit on his dick."

He eyeballed Angells, who knew that the DCI would not have dared to make that comment if the super had still been in the room. Angells returned his gaze for a full five seconds, resisted the temptation to comment explicitly on Fortune's knowledge of gay jargon and the reference to himself, and said, only slightly less calmly than usual, "That's correct, sir. Sergeant Kahn has been dealin' with the club, so, unless there are questions, I'll pass over to him."

* * *

Ross

With Raith, it was different from the way it had been

with Phil. As well as our house, there were five other houses in our little Tunhead terrace plus, as I said, a big, dilapidated storehouse. Perhaps I didn't say it was dilapidated. There was also a ruined detached cottage and another little terrace—six houses—on the other side of the street, by the storehouse. At the height of the quarrying, Tunhead was big enough for a little church as well. It serviced the little farms and other cottages strung out along Tun Beck. It's still consecrated, actually, though it's only used occasionally now.

Now there's no work in quarrying, the whole area's so rundown you can get places for next to nothing. Mike and I bought the house next door to ours, and the storehouse, for a pittance. I think the owners of the other houses hoped to rent them out as holiday lets, but it didn't happen, and now we have the whole of the hamlet for ourselves. We bought the cottage too. We gutted everything, refurbished, and rented the spaces to friends and colleagues of mine. Potters, painters, sculptors, jewellery makers, who didn't mind being out in the middle of nowhere. Raith was one.

I knew he liked Mike, knew it pretty quickly. I'd watch Raith looking at him, and I knew he was stripping him of every piece of clothing, one garment at a time, picturing licking skin as he laid each long limb and flexing muscle bare. If he did nothing about it, it wasn't to spare my feelings. It was because he had a long-time partner.

For as long as I'd known Raith, there'd been Peri, Raith's model. French. Good looking, possessive, jealous, and as wild as Raith himself, though in a different way. His name's Pierre, Pierre Lescaut, but we called him Peri. Not because it's an Anglo-French gay pun—'peri' being French for 'fairy'. It was simply that Raith saw the letters written and got them mixed up the way he always does. If I were the Queen of the Fairies though (sorry, that one *is* embarrassing), I'd have stripped him of his powers and banished him to a place where he could do no harm.

I could never quite get a handle on their relationship. Raith's a big, aggressive guy, and I know that I shouldn't fall prey to a stereotype, especially an LGBTQ one, but if you'd have asked me, I'd have definitely said that Raith was dom. Yet he'd sometimes appear with a bruised cheek or a bust lip, and I had the feeling it wasn't due to a bit of S and M that had got out of hand. Then, three years ago, they had a huge bust-up, and Peri returned to France—as far as we knew, for good. He came back, but that's getting ahead of the game.

When Peri left, Raith didn't exactly move in, but he didn't just occupy his own place either. He'd often eat with us. His washing would turn up in our basket. He'd add little drawings to the shopping list pinned up on the wall. (I should have kept those lists. They'd be worth money—which would go some way to paying for the food he ate.) In the end, I put my foot down, and that's when we decided to have a rota and a few rules. I mean, if Raith was going to leave his paint-splattered, clay-infested overalls next to my underpants then he could at least hang the bloody things out on the washing line afterwards. And if he was going to help himself to the food in our freezer, then he could at least replace the fish fingers occasionally.

And I said all this to Raith, getting hot under the collar, and Mike just sat there with that knowing look and a little smile playing round his fucking gorgeous mouth, and his eyes laughing. Saying nothing and just letting Raith and me sort it out, which, to give us our due, through the 'T' word (talking), we did. But, do you know what? I'd have had not just Raith Balan but the whole of Raith Rovers bloody football team living in the house if Mike had wanted. I love the man to bits, and I know now that no one could love me as much as he does. I needn't have worried about losing him to Raith. Nor to Phil, as it happened. I should have paid more attention to Peri.

Chapter 6

Flaxby came out of Fortune's office looking thoughtful. A few minutes later, he called Angells on an internal line.

"We've got a lead in the Coverham case, Mike," he said with a surprising lack of enthusiasm. "Come in here first opp, will you?"

"What is it, sir?" asked Angells, five minutes later.

Flaxby hesitated.

"You sent some photos off to Gateshead in case this lad we're looking for in the Coverham case frequents the Metro Centre there."

"That's right."

"Gateshead have just called back. They had a response from the people at Cinderella's."

"Oh?" Angells said cautiously. Cinderella's used to have a name that was all too familiar to him.

"The staff think they've recognised our missing man. He often goes to the Saturday late-nighters, though he always leaves early, apparently. I want you over there chasing it up," Flaxby added apologetically.

"Aw, come on, Clive," Angells said anxiously. On duty, he nearly always addressed the super with the respect due to rank. It took strong emotion to let the 'sir' slip and, even then, it only happened out of other people's hearing. "Why can't someone from Gateshead go? Cinders is theirs, not ours."

"I know that, Mike, but the dead lad's ours and if this other one is too, it'll be thrown back at us anyway. You know that."

"But there's surely someone else who can check it out. Doesn't have to be me, does it? You know I've got problems with Cinders. It used to be Emelda's. You know that."

"I do know, yes."

"Then why?"

"Two reasons, Mike. One, I don't have anybody else except the DCI, and there's no way I can send him to a gay nightclub, neither undercover nor out of it. Two, even if I had someone, which I don't, you are the best person to send. You know that."

Flaxby waited. Sensing Angells' resignation, he pushed his point and continued. "Contact them and make some arrangement to go there this Saturday evening. Take Sunny Sanghera with you."

"Sunny? You're jokin', sir," said Angells incredulously. Sandeep Sanghera was as straight a guy as any on the TTW force. The idea of him being undercover in a gay nightclub needed nearly as much imagination as did the thought of Chief Inspector Fortune doing likewise.

"It'll be an education for him," said the super.

"For both of us, I reckon. Sir, is there nuthin' I can do to get out of this? Nuthin' at all?"

Flaxby shook his head apologetically.

Angells sighed. "OK. I'll phone Cinders in a bit and make some arrangements for Saturday night. But I don't want to," he added dispiritedly.

"Thanks, Mike. I know this is hard for you," said Flaxby. "Look, it's midday and I could do with a pint. Come on, man. Come for a drink and a bite to eat and sort out Cinderella's afterwards. Come on. On me," he added encouragingly, seeing the misery in his inspector's face. *Maybe a pint of brown'll loosen his tongue, and I can figure out what's troubling him,* he thought. *There's something, that's for sure.*

But whatever it was, a pint of brown ale wasn't enough to bring it to the surface.

* * *

So it was that the straightest and the gayest of Warbridge's CID went on what most people, well out of the inspector's hearing, called a date. The PCs and DCs seemed to find the situation uproariously amusing, and everyone seemed to have at least one piece of unrequested advice for poor DC Sanghera.

The DC himself began with a question.

"Sir," he said, when he managed to find Angells alone, "what shall I wear?"

"Clothes might be good," said Angells.

"Yes, but what sort of clothes? What's the dress code?" the DC persisted.

"You mean: should you go in sumthin' pink and frilly?"

Sanghera looked aghast.

"Or would you be better with a leather thong and nuthin' else? Wouldn't try that. Only one place for your warrant card."

"Sir, please," Sanghera said imploringly, uncertain if Angells was joking or not. "I've never even stuck my head inside a gay nightclub on duty, let alone this."

"It is on duty," Angells said firmly.

"Yes, I know. I meant called out to a fight or sumthin'. I don't know what to expect, that's all."

Angells wondered why attending a fight in a gay club would be any different from attending a fight in any other, but he simply said, "I know, Sunny. Look, I haven't been to Emelda's—I mean Cinderella's—for a long time, so I don't quite know, but if it's like other places that I do know, then smart casual's fine, I reckon. We've got to come back here with this guy, don't forget, so I wouldn't be too OTT."

"No. I wasn't plannin' to be. *If* he comes, though."

"Aye. *If* he comes. But you'd better not call me 'sir'."

"No, sir. What then, sir?"

For sure, not Angel Baby! He didn't really want Sanghera to call him 'Mike' in case, not thinking, he slipped into first name familiarity at the station. There was protocol to consider, and he knew it could cause the young DC embarrassment if, forgetting himself, he addressed Angells as 'Mike' in front of his peers. Well he'd have to take a chance on Sanghera remembering where he was.

"Mike," he said, and followed it with, "So what have they been tellin' you to find out?"

"Who, sir?"

Angells nodded in the direction of the CID room.

"What flavour sponkies I like? Whether I go top or bottom?"

Sanghera blushed. *Those and a whole pile of other things*, he thought. *Like what sort of piercings do you have, and are you covered in whip marks?*

"Take no notice," Angells said, "but they'll want to know all about it when they get in on Monday. You can bet on that. And they'll want to see the photos, too."

He smiled, so Sanghera nodded and ventured a smile himself.

"Shall I meet you here?" he asked.

"What? In all your pink fluffy finery? You'll get locked up! I'll pick you up at home if that's OK. Away from pryin' eyes."

"Thanks, sir. What about money?"

"Don't worry. On account."

Concern must have still shown in the young man's face, for the inspector added, "Don't worry, eh? It's just work."

That's what he'd have to keep on reminding himself.

* * *

Sanghera was pleasantly surprised when Angells knocked on the door of his lodgings at eight o'clock that Saturday night. He'd half expected him to arrive in his tightest leathers, perhaps replete with gold neck chain and possibly an earring or two. Instead, the inspector looked positively normal— well-cut, dark green polycotton trousers, pale green open-necked shirt and a lightweight biker-style jacket the colour of the ground turmeric in Sanghera's mother's spice rack. Apart from a gold wristwatch, not a bit of bling in sight. It was only when they were driving that Sanghera noticed that Angells had replaced his wedding ring with an even broader signet ring. Same finger (to cover up the paler flesh?) but implying no significant relationship between the two of them.

Thank goodness. Not that he's bad looking—for his age, Sanghera decided. Angells had blossomed early, but, though now well into his thirties, he was showing no signs of dropping his blooms.

It had been a good three quarters of an hour's

drive from Tunhead back towards Warbridge to collect Sanghera, and it was a further hour or more to Cinderella's. The last half an hour passed in total silence. Angells was uncommunicative and the DC, who could have chatted garrulously about the pros and cons of various sports cars, found himself unable to whip up any enthusiasm for the Ford Fiesta they were travelling in. *Strange how a speed freak like the inspector should own so conventional a car, even a souped-up one,* he thought, not realising how, to a biker like Angells, two wheels offered freedom and a race with the wind, four wheels merely a means of bringing home the shopping in a single journey or, as now, the means to ferry a passenger to an unwelcome destination.

The constable amused himself by wondering if his superior had ever broken any rules. They'd kept precisely to the speed limit the whole way, even slowing to the requisite twenty when they'd driven through a residential area. *Perhaps he's programmed to abide by the law of the land,* Sanghera mused. *You shall not neglect to obey any statute or code, or part thereof, enshrined by Act of Parliament or local bylaw, on pain of death.*

In fact, Angells had driven, not so much on auto-pilot—he always gave the road his attention—but in a frame of mind that allowed him to perform two tasks with equal attentiveness. He drove with awareness whilst thinking of a man he'd once loved and of another Saturday night. If Sanghera had been aware of the story replaying in the inspector's head, he would have understood and respected the silence.

Finally, engrossed in their various musings, they arrived. Angells smoothly and neatly parked the car and, after a huge sigh which Sanghera interpreted purely as fatigue, spoke quietly to a hefty looking doorman who immediately spoke on his mobile, and the two detectives went inside.

Sanghera's first impressions were that Cinderella's was just like any other club on a Saturday night—bizarrely colourful under the curving sweep of ceiling lights, dark and full of shadows otherwise. Busy and noisy, especially in the loos, where the variety of toiletries on offer—hairsprays, mousses, gels, aftershaves, and a veritable bonanza of smellies and related products—was the only thing that made Cinderella's any different from other clubs Sanghera knew.

Angells pointed to a spot at the side of the dance floor from where they could see both the doors and the bar. Sanghera wondered if they were in for a night standing up. Dancing even, God help him. However, a member of staff brought over a small table and two chairs, quickly followed by glasses, two bottles of apple and raspberry juice and two of the passion fruit juice that Angells knew the young DC drank in the police station canteen.

"Help yourself," said Angells, and withdrew into a silence so fierce that his young colleague didn't dare to break it, not that he could think of anything to say.

* * *

"So what did happen?" asked nearly every other PC and DC in the station on the following Monday.

Sanghera gave the longest answer to DC Sally Topley, mainly because given the choice of a date with her, with Angells or with anyone else in Warbridge station, he'd definitely choose her.

"What happened? Not an awful lot," he said. "I mean, here, you can talk about a case, but there, we couldn't. Didn't want the clubbers to overhear obviously. So he was all remote and morose, and I was thinkin' of all the things I could be doin' on a Saturday night."

"It wasn't the height of fun then?" Sally Topley said.

"Not even the low of fun. I mean, what do you talk about socially when you're sat at a table with a gay superior officer and you can't talk shop?"

"I'm surprised nobody tried to pick you up. Good looker like you!"

"Oh aye? Thanks. One fella did actually. Dressed head to foot in red silk and asked if I wanted a dance. So the inspector says, 'He's with me,' and sticks his arm firmly around my shoulders to emphasise his point. Red Silk looks at his face, and the state of his biceps, and says sorry and moves off. Shame really. It would probably have been more entertainin'."

"I'm sure if you'd had to stay longer you'd have had more offers," Topley said, mock consolation in her voice.

"Thank you. It was bad enough when he put his arm round me. I think I flinched, cos then he said sorry to me. I felt a bit mean then, cos for all he can be hard to work for, he's a good guy, isn't he?"

"Very."

Both spent a moment recalling times when they had been very grateful to Angells indeed.

"So then the suspect came in?" said Topley, returning to the present—or, rather, to the present of two evenings past.

"That's right. The DI had arranged with the bar staff to keep a lookout for him and to bring drinks over to us so we wouldn't lose our seats.

Then it was sheepdog trials time: I skirt the room clockwise, he skirts it anti, and we converge on this guy and pen him in."

"Did he need penning in?"

"Not really, but he was by the door and we didn't want him runnin' out on us again. He looked at the DI, who is doing the ID thing, and he looked at me and he looked relieved. It was that 'I knew I'd be found out and I'm almost glad I have been' look."

Topley nodded her recognition.

"So he came along to the station like a lamb to the slaughter," said Sanghera.

"And was there slaughter?"

"There was sumthin', but it wasn't slaughter, no."

Some straightforward questions, initially from Sanghera to put the man at ease. His name was Thijs Falconer, first name pronounced 'Tice.' Yes, it was an unusual name, in England anyway. He'd been born in Winchester, but his mum was Dutch and the family had lived in the Netherlands, in Utrecht, until his mother died. Then he'd come north east with his dad, who was from Sunderland originally. Twenty-three years old, and he lived in Warbridge. Yes, he had a UK passport not a Dutch one. No, he didn't have a regular job. Not since leaving uni a year or so ago. He'd studied video and film production.

Yes, he'd been to Manny's Bar the afternoon that John Coverham died, but he hadn't known about the death until he'd seen the news that evening. Honestly! He'd swear it! And, yes, he knew the victim well. John Coverham was his lover. He'd met him through his dad who was the accountant for the club, for Ormerley. John and he had been lovers for the past three years, and that was what they'd been arguing about. The fact that he had wanted John to come out and stop keeping their relationship secret, but John wouldn't. So they'd been arguing and rowing and arguing and rowing all day, and when John had walked, furious, into the lav, he'd followed to reason with him, but he hadn't touched him and he didn't know any more than that. He'd run because he was upset, not because he was trying to get away from a crime. He'd calmed down by the time he got to Raneleigh Street, and he'd caught the bus home.

He hadn't gone to Cinders to pull, if that's what they thought. As though John Coverham didn't matter. That's where he often went when John had a home match. Then John would text him and he'd get a taxi back to his place. He'd gone because… He didn't really know why he'd gone. Just to get out of the house. Just to put something else in his mind. Just because the man he loved was dead, and to go somewhere and think of something else.

Sanghera continued his questioning, the DI apparently listening closely before, as was his custom, taking a more active role himself.

Suddenly, Thijs Falconer clammed up as though it had dawned on him that he was making a statement in a police station, in a small room with two non-uniformed cops and a third, in uniform, standing at the door. The oldest of the three, the non-uniformed one who hadn't spoken much, looked as though he ate gay men for breakfast. If Falconer's gaydar had been half as good as Ross Whitburn's, he'd have realised how wrong his assessment of Angells was.

Angells stopped the tape and asked the uniformed constable to bring in some tea and coffee. He had to ask himself who precisely it was for—the man they were interviewing or himself. The lad was describing one situation that he'd known all too well and another—he realised with relief—he had never had to suffer.

On the one hand, he understood Thijs Falconer's pain: he knew everything there was to know about grief. God knows, in a sense he was still grieving, but on the other hand he was thinking how lucky he was. How would he have acted if he'd joined the force ten, even five, years earlier than he had done? Would he have joined? It was hard enough to deal complacently with one man's—Fortune's—evil volleys. Not too long ago, he'd have been faced with a whole company of similar-minded bigots. Then what would he have done? Perhaps exactly what John Coverham had felt he had to do: lived behind a secret. And what would that have done to his relationship with Ross, or before Ross, with Sam? Might they, like Falconer, have spent their time complaining they were sick and tired of skulking in corners, of keeping the relationship hidden inside four walls, of never going clubbing, of never doing anything that would jeopardise Angells' job?

Thank God Ross and Raith and Phil aren't secretive, he thought. Phil especially, in a way, as people's expectations of artists and surgeons were, illogically, rather different. *Thank God their openness means I can be open too.*

So there was a lengthy pause while two of the four people present regained their composure. Then the detectives ran through everything again, the only difference being that, this time, Angells asked the questions and the DC listened to the answers. The point was that Coverham had banged his head somehow, and as far as Angells and Sanghera could see, the only person who could have caused him to do so was the man in front of them. No matter how they put this to Falconer, he maintained that he hadn't done anything except argue. For all his mangled emotions, he was sticking to his story and doing so despite facing one of the most perceptive interviewers in the whole of the TTW Force. That was no mean feat.

Angells nodded to Sanghera to stop the tape again, and the two men went outside.

"Well?" asked Angells.

"There's something, isn't there, sir?"

Angells nodded. He'd felt that too.

"I mean," Sanghera explained, "it was word for word the same story second time round. That's not right. Like he'd learnt it."

"I know," said Angells uneasily.

The professional thing to do was take another break then see if the story held a third time round. But Angells was physically and emotionally drained, and visibly tired, and he could hardly keep his eyes open, let alone think straight. He'd done a full day's work. He'd driven home, driven back, gone to Gateshead, returned to Warbridge. Definitely Phil's that night. He couldn't face another drive.

"Look, I think we have to let him go for now. He's still in the frame, obviously, but we can bring him in again, on the pretext of a rep for wastin' our time and not comin' forward if we've nuthin' else, but I can't see how we can keep him here tonight."

Sanghera simply said, "OK, sir. Whatever you think. Like you say, we can get him back any time."

Or at least they thought they could.

* * *

Phil

It doesn't seem as though I saw him first ten years or so ago. He was still dressed for clubbing, of course. Attractively dressed too, in clothes that displayed his strong upper body and good long legs to perfection. I was attracted to him. I quite fancied those legs wrapped around my junior doctor's midriff, and I'd have liked nothing more than to put a consoling arm around his shoulders. I'm proud to say I didn't. I simply told him I was very sorry, but I doubt he heard. He stayed in my mind for a long time. A big strong cop sobbing his heart out for his dead lover.

Anyway, I was working in Gateshead General, and I gathered he was working somewhere further south, so it looked as though our paths would never cross again.

Probably because I'm gay, I thought that there might be a career in anal sex. No, I don't mean that I saw myself earning my living by renting out my bum, but anal sex can cause some really nasty tears. That's tears as in cuts, not tears as in crying, though it sometimes does that too, believe me! I began to be involved in the whole area of rectal repair. That probably sounds a gruesome term but it's faster to say than rectal reconstruction.

At the uni in Warbridge, one of the departments was involved in nanocarbon research. I could see potential medical uses: not just to repair a rectum damaged by rough sex, but rectal cancer, for example. To shorten the story, I moved to Warbridge in order to liaise with the uni, and to specialise in the work at the city hospital. The police were often in and out, and one day, there he was. A few years older, just as sexy, and to my surprise, he remembered me. Over a cup of coffee in the hospital canteen, he told me what had happened between then and now. How he'd met Ross.

How they'd gradually bought the whole of Tunhead, a deserted quarry village at the head of Tun Beck, a tributary of the Wear. How Ross had turned it into BOTWAC, the Beck on the Wear Arts Centre. He was laughing as he told me this, grey-green eyes full of laughter. Apparently, they regularly received enquiries from people hoping for a secluded week of B and D.

"I had to go with BOTWAC," he said. "I couldn't let him name it after where we live, could I? It'd be TOTWAC then!"

And I realised what a neat accent he had. You'd say, "North East," but you'd have to be from somewhere hereabouts to distinguish Geordie from Macca or Bishop from Barnard Castle. There are more accents than closed collieries in this part of the world. His accent was slight, but he had all the northern vowels and an alphabet of twenty five and a half letters: there were 'g's within and at the start of words, but I've never heard him put one at the end of a word. And 'was'—always 'wuz'. So "I was looking in the window," would emerge as "A wuz luckin' in the windor." But lightly and softly. South Durham. No way Tyneside and "Haway the lads!"

So he'd moved on, obviously, and he wasn't living in the past, but—and this was the big 'but'—a part of him was still raw.

"Even after all these years," he said, "and even though I love Ross to bits, I can never forget how I felt when Sam died in that ambulance. I still have nightmares about it. Regularly. I've seen so many dead bodies and I've stood there when people have cried—or been too shocked to cry—and I know how they feel and I know that there's not a single bloody thing you can do about it. No magic wand. No magic words. No nuthin'. If sumthin' like that happened to Ross, I don't know what I'd do. Twice! God, no. Not twice. I couldn't bear to lose Ross."

Chapter 7

Inspector Angells was driving to the station to start his shift, a few days after he and Sanghera had interviewed Falconer, when his car was overtaken by an ambulance and a marked police car, both with sirens blaring. He wondered what the emergency was, and switched his radio to his police wavelength in order to find out. It transpired that a driver had spun into oncoming vehicles in an effort to miss two pedestrians pushing a pram over a pedestrian crossing. The driver, the young couple and their baby were all unhurt, but a passenger in one of the smashed vehicles was seriously injured. The ambulance Angells had seen was rushing the badly injured woman to the hospital.

Procedure required that the driver who skidded should be interviewed at the station as soon as possible. Angells entered just as the man was being taken to an interview room. Their eyes met, briefly, though Angells continued staring. There was no recognition on the driver's side, but Angells' jaw dropped open in surprise. He recognised the driver.

"Who's doin' the interview, Jay?" he asked the duty sergeant.

"O'Neill, I think. Looks like this idiot was usin' his mobile. One lady in A&E, an' a young couple and their little 'un could've 'ended up there too. Stupid bloody bugger."

"Do you think she'd mind if I sat in?"

"Ask her. Here she is."

It seemed a strange request for CID to make, but Sergeant O'Neill agreed that the DI could sit in on the interview if he wanted to.

Angells sat and listened as the driver tried to wriggle out of the charges O'Neill suggested would be brought against him. He was adamant he hadn't been on his phone, but the log showed recent use and an abruptly ended call. Moreover, a GoPro camera fixed to the dashboard of a stationary taxi showed him racing past, even though the lights ahead were red and the couple with the pram already crossing.

The man became aware of Angells watching him. Such scrutiny made him feel uncomfortable. He couldn't understand why this plain-clothes cop was sitting there, or why he was looking at him so intensely. The cop was as still as a statue. He was just watching. Why?

At that moment, Angells was meant to be reporting to Flaxby. The super phoned the desk.

"Hasn't Angells got in yet?" he asked. Angells' arrival by bike was obvious, but he made far less noise by car.

"Aye, sir. He's sitting in with Sergeant O'Neill on a traffic."

"What for?" asked Flaxby with puzzled irritation. "Who is it they're interviewing?"

"Man by the name of Taylor Collingwood," said the duty sergeant innocently. He was about to add that Collingwood had previous form for traffic violations, but the phone had gone dead and Flaxby was racing down the stairs.

He pulled open the shutter on the interview

room door and looked inside. The inspector was side on to him. His posture appeared relaxed but Flaxby, a pro who could read all the signs, looked at the rise and fall of Angells' chest and knew he was looking at another pro, someone masking great emotion by forcing himself to breathe deeply in order to relax and give the lie of calm. Angells glanced up: he'd heard the shutter move. Briefly, their gazes met, then Angells' eyes returned to the man who sat opposite the sergeant at the table.

Flaxby walked back to the duty desk.

"Tell the inspector I want to see him the moment that interview is finished," he ordered. "Make sure he knows."

A quarter of an hour later, Angells knocked on the super's door, heard, "Yes?" and went in. He sat down after, once again, shifting a pile of folders and paperwork from the chair.

"It was him, wasn't it?" said Superintendent Flaxby. He didn't really require either confirmation or an answer, for it wasn't really a question.

"Yes," was all the inspector said.

"Did he recognise you?"

"No. Why should he remember me? I'm forgettable. Just someone who…" He didn't complete his sentence. Just swallowed and shook his head slightly. "As soon as I saw him, I knew. You were on that case, weren't you, sir?"

"I recognised the name, yes. That was the case that made me decide that if ever I made super, I wanted cops like you working in my division."

"What? Gay cops?" Angells said incredulously.

"No. Cops acquainted with grief. Who are hard—we have to be hard—but not so hard we forget about feelings. You know the number of times we have to knock on a door and give folk bad news. They know if the words we're using are hollow. Recitations from a manual. Genuine concern. Small comfort maybe, but sometimes, small comforts are all we can offer folk."

Angells nodded his understanding and sighed. Then a humbling thought hit him.

"Are you sayin' it's not just a coincidence I ended up in Warbridge? You picked me, a bit like the draft in American football?"

"A bit, but don't get big-headed. I didn't have much competition. There was more than one who said, 'You know he's gay, don't you?' I told 'em that as long as you did your job, you could be a two-headed alien with six legs and a tail for all I cared. Thank God we've passed the days when you had to keep schtum or be chucked out as too soft or a blackmail risk."

"Thank you, sir. Thank you. I won't let you down."

"You'd better not. You'll wish you weren't born if you do!" It didn't sound like an empty threat.

Angells' thoughts returned to Collingwood. "I've never sought him out," he said after a pause. "I could've. I mean, I never felt he got what he deserved."

"But you didn't. Cos you're a cop, not a vigilante."

"There's a part of me wishes I was. I mean— the fact that he didn't recognise me. It means he doesn't think about it, doesn't it? Not haunted by faces from the past. No remorse."

"Maybe."

"I'd've liked him to remember me. I'd've felt there was some justice in the world if he'd remembered. Maybe I've just aged a lot." A half-hearted joke. "You know what I mean though, don't you?"

"Oh, yes," said Flaxby knowingly. "But, Mike,

we just get them to the courts. That's our part of the job done. There's some that, as you want, will think about it, and there's some that won't. You know how it works. But it's still worthwhile, doing the job. Because of the ones who will."

"You don't reckon it's about keepin' people off the streets then?"

"Yes, but that's a different thing. Protecting society, not punishing offenders. For punishment, I'm inclined to think like you. The best—or, rather, the worst—punishments happen in the mind. You pay your dues for life, not just the term of your sentence."

"Mmm. Not in Taylor Collingwood's case, obviously." Angells sighed again. "Have you ever wanted to smash someone senseless, sir?"

"I'm sure we all have. You know the type of case. But as I say, it isn't what we do and it *is* a sure-fire way to lose your job."

Angells nodded.

"Is that what you wanted to do when you saw who it was?" asked Flaxby. "Smash him senseless?"

"No. I've never wanted to. Wouldn't change nuthin', would it?"

There was work to be getting on with, but Flaxby ignored it. His priority was sorting out the man seated before him.

"How are the Angel Band doing?" he asked, abruptly changing the subject.

"Sir?" Angells looked bewildered. Then the penny dropped and he laughed. "Is that what you and Mrs Flaxby call us?" he asked. "The Angel Band?"

The super's wife was a competent amateur potter with what, she'd tell Flaxby, was 'insider knowledge' of the goings on at BOTWAC.

"It's what Mrs F. calls the four of you, yes. I tell her that you're more a den of devils, but she won't have it. She's even thinking of booking in for a pottery weekend."

"She should, sir!" Angells said enthusiastically. "She'd have a great time. And at the end of the activity weekends, there's always a big party and a display of what people have done."

"As long as that's all that's displayed, then!"

"Sir!"

"To be honest, I just think she'd like to turn your Raith Balan. Fat chance, with you in the red corner!"

"And Phil in the blue. Don't forget Phil."

The super waited while the second penny dropped.

"I'm so happy there—with the Angel Band, as you call us. I love 'em to bits—that sometimes I feel I'm lettin'—"

"Mike," the super interrupted, "you can be loyal to a memory and still move on. For God's sake, man, don't beat yourself up for enjoying the present and for living in it."

Angells considered this. "I know. And I do live in the present."

"Just as well," said Flaxby, pointing to the pile of paperwork surrounding him and bringing the discussion to what he hoped was a suitably positive close. "I thought computers were supposed to help us with efficiency, not hinder us. Let's try and get through some of this lot, shall we? So, firstly, how did you get on yesterday?"

While this impromptu counselling session was taking place, the man who had caused it, Taylor Collingwood, was completing various formalities prior to leaving the station. He was one of those people with an exceptionally poor memory for faces: a useless picker-out at an identity parade. He could remember names, though.

"That man who just sat there," he said, "who was he?"

"CID inspector. Michael Angells," said the sergeant.

A third penny dropped and Collingwood turned pale. "Oh hell," he said. "Shit."

Sergeant O'Neill looked at him.

"Did he used to ride a bike? Motorbike?"

"Still does," she said.

"Will you tell him something?"

O'Neill wondered what he might have to say to Angells and simply waited.

"Tell him, if it means anything, I do think about what happened. I might be stupid enough to text while I'm driving, but I'm not so stupid that I'm drunk when I'm doing it."

He left before O'Neill could think of a reply.

"What was that about?" she asked the duty sergeant.

"I don't know," he said, "but you might as well pass the message on."

She did so an hour or so later.

"Thank you," Angells said. He slowly continued on his way, thinking about the implications of Collingwood's message.

* * *

Ross

Raith's work's a real money-spinner. I can sell an original painting for a few thousand, and I've buyers for his sculptures who'll pay enough to keep him in clay and acrylics for life. He's serious about his art, but he's got a great sense of humour too and, fortunately, so has Mike. Mike can be quite frivolous when he wants! Hence 'The Pastoral Series'. I suggested it, and Mike and Raith loved the idea. There was one proviso: Mike was to stay incognito.

"Can you imagine what would happen," he had said, "if I went to collar some crook and there's a paintin' of me in the buff hangin' over the fireplace! I'd die of shame."

Usually, though, 'The Pastoral Series' finds its way into houses as calendars, cards and tea towels. If Raith can't manage to hide Mike's face behind a surreal assortment of flora and fauna, he turns it coyly away from the viewer. So far, Mike's anonymity has been successfully preserved! And so, to my continual delight, one can buy Mike languidly lying on a bed of lilac heather; Mike, wet and sparkly, washing in a rush-lined pool; Mike dallying with a daisy chain as he leans lazily against a rustic gate; Mike, seated seductively on a river bank, tickling his toes in the water, and, of course, Mike sprawled sleepily but sexily across the birthday card that he knows Chief Inspector Fortune bought for his wife's birthday. Mike happened to glimpse it peeping out of some files lying on the chief inspector's desk. If the CI only knew!

Chapter 8

Though not a particularly introspective man, Angells had an opportunity the following day to inspect and analyse his feelings more thoroughly. He and DC Topley were sitting in the draughty station canteen having a well-earned break. They'd discussed the weather (windy and cold, hence the draught), the sports results (worse), the state of British politics (appalling) and were now onto the ease with which a person could acquire celebrity status.

"Five minutes of fame, then it's back to oblivion," said Topley. "Though I wouldn't say no to the five minutes."

Angells smiled.

"Aye," he said. "Mind you, up at Tunhead, we've got Raith, and he's had far more than five minutes of telly and stuff. The media love him. He ticks lots of their boxes."

"How do you mean?"

"Well… reformed criminal—so he says—lots of talent—so he says—proof you can be successful and dyslexic, mixed-race parentage, gay—well, much more gay than bi—and he'll talk for England if you let him."

"Where *is* he from?"

"Leamington Spa."

"Leamington Spa? Really?"

"Really. But his parents are from Barranquilla in Colombia and he's not entirely sure why they left. He thinks they had to. His dad looks like my idea of a Spanish aristocrat, I suppose. Very distinguished. Like the portraits of the military who commanded the Armada. His mam's got some African—West African, I think. From way back, I'd say. His features are more like his dad's. His colourin's more his mam's. He's got three brothers, but two of 'em are the other way round. They're all of 'em strappin'."

"Are they all named after Scottish football teams? Hamilton Balan?"

"Montrose Balan."

"Forfar Balan."

"Dundee United Balan."

"Stirling Albion Balan." She was going to say "Queen of the South Balan", but stopped herself just in time.

"No." Angells laughed. "He got his name because they wanted one that sounded English!"

"They got their geography a bit wrong then, didn't they?"

"Mm, but apparently there isn't a 'th' sound in their version of Spanish, and when they heard the football scores…"

"Good job they didn't go with Cowdenbeath then! You've obviously met them?"

"Often. They're great. His mam told me they tore their hair out over him when he was in his teens, but now they feel really proud. Not *of* him. *For* him. Ross loves puttin' on his work."

"Ross is your partner, right?"

"Yes."

But whether the inspector felt that the conversation had become too personal, or whether it was simply the fact that his thoughts were leading him elsewhere, he volunteered no further details, and fixed his clear gaze on a potted plant that was quivering on a draughty window ledge.

He was thinking of his conversation with the super the previous day, and the fact that if he had moved on from Sam Mitford's death, his progress was in no small measure due to Ross.

What has Ross done for me? he asked himself, purposely parodying the title of a book and television series. *Everything!*

That first dinner they'd had. Ross had suggested a country house restaurant located a few miles north of Newcastle. He was obviously known there.

"The artwork on the walls," he said, "it's some of the ones I can't sell. I let them have it cheap!"

However, the main reason why he had chosen that particular restaurant was that he knew Mike would have to sleep over. He wasn't sure where Tunhead was, but he knew it was somewhere distant and remote—probably too far for Mike to travel home to. So Mike had driven to the restaurant in his car, together with an overnight bag, but had insisted—somewhat forcefully, it seemed to Ross—that Ross should arrive by taxi, they'd take a taxi back to Ross's apartment, and next morning, either Ross or another taxi would drive Mike back to the restaurant car park. No drinking and driving. Not even a drop.

The food was good, the service impeccable, and no one looked twice at the fact that two men were dining together over a meal that clearly wasn't a business one. They enjoyed each other's conversation and descriptions of mishaps at work, and Ross had made it perfectly clear that, as the one who'd done the inviting, he'd pick up the bill—"On condition," he said, "that you pick up the next one."

There'll be a next one! Smashin', thought Mike.

So, laughing and chatting like old friends, they took a taxi back to Ross's. They both knew how the plumbing worked. They sealed their friendship with much more than a kiss.

It was on their fourth or fifth meeting that Angells had said, "There's sumthin' you ought to know. I'm tellin' you cos if you think I'm a total loony and you'd rather not see me again then I'd rather it happened now, before I become so fond of you that… I dunno. I'm already fond of you." Then he stopped speaking.

Ross was on the point of jokingly saying that he didn't have ESP when he saw that, whatever it was, it wasn't a joking matter. He did what he became very good at doing. He clasped one of Mike's hands in both of his own, and waited.

"Well," he said, after Mike had completed a hesitant explanation, "are you a skilful cook?"

"Cook? I can put a ready meal in the microwave and open a tin of beans."

"Not the beans, but the other will do. You get the food, I'll get the wine, and next time we meet, we'll eat at your house and you can show me the graveyard."

"You mean there could still be a next time, despite what I've just told you? You're not bothered?"

"I won't say it's not unusual," said Ross. He looked at Angells' face. "Do you still love him?" he asked gently, correctly reading the hope lodged in Mike's grey-green eyes and confident he knew the answer. "You think about him, but do you still love him?"

"No."

"Could you love me?"

"I already do."

"Then of course there'll be a next time."

And the next time was wonderful.

Mike opened the front door. Ross couldn't hide his astonishment.

"Are we still on Planet Earth?" he asked. "This is plain ridiculous. You really drive here every night?"

"Sometimes I ride. That's my bike." Mike pointed.

"You ride to Warbridge police station? In full leathers?"

"Yes."

"Even in winter?"

"Sometimes."

"But there aren't any streetlights. It must be pitch black by four o'clock!"

"Aye, it is. In winter."

"You *are* loony! And who lives in the other houses?" asked Ross, laughing. He removed his jacket and hung it over the banister on the stairs. "Vampires?"

"There's probably a few bats and owls," said Mike, "but I don't think there are any vampires. Don't you like it?" he asked, visibly disappointed.

"Like it? I think it's bloody wonderful! I didn't know places like this still existed."

Later, as they finished off their 'Dine in for two for £10' meal and immediately felt the need to begin a second, Ross asked, "Seriously, don't you get just a bit scared? It's so isolated."

"I'm a cop!" laughed Mike. "I'm scared of loonies carryin' guns and crowbars and six-inch knives, but I'm not scared of my imagination! I stand more chance of bein' attacked by some idiot swingin' a baseball bat in Warbridge town centre than bein' attacked by sumthin' round here. Mind you, first time I heard an owl shriek, I thought it *was* someone gettin' attacked. I went racin' into the street in my nuddy!"

"Were any people in the holiday homes? If they'd have looked out of the window, they'd have thought *you* were the attacker." Ross laughed.

"If there were, they looked the other way."

"Fools! I'd have been out there taking photos or performing a citizen's arrest—decent exposure."

"*In*decent exposure," corrected Mike.

"Think about it!"

He did, and sheepishly smiled.

"Come on," said Ross. "All this talk of owls and things that go bump in the night. Show me the graveyard."

"Now?"

"Very much now. You're not going to really relax until you've shown me and I've shown you I'm OK with it," said Ross, standing up.

Mike sighed.

"OK. I'd grab your jacket, though. It gets nippy on the hillside."

"Right, lay on, Macduff," Ross briskly said, adding softly, as he turned to retrieve his jacket from the banister, "Let's go and confront your demons."

Ross followed Mike past the other houses and along a cobbled track that led from the top of the hamlet to the little church. The graveyard was somewhat untidy and overgrown, but a few of the graves were still well tended, and Mike guided Ross to one. Just a simple inscription on the headstone and the comment "Resting peacefully."

It struck Ross that, whilst the description

"resting peacefully" might apply to the dead man, it didn't seem to apply to the man who remained quick. He had a dozen questions he wanted to ask—mundane ones, awkward ones, practical ones—but he knew that there'd be plenty of time to ask them. He didn't need answers right now. He placed an arm around Mike's waist and waited. He felt he might have to do a lot of waiting for someone who, he could see, was struggling to leave the past behind, but Ross knew that he could be patient. He knew he *would* be patient: the man beside him would be worth the wait.

"This whole churchyard needs a damn good tidy up," Ross said eventually. "Come the better weather, I'll help you do it."

He did more than that. He brought the whole of Tunhead back to life. Three years later, it was unrecognisable—full of activity and laughter, with streetlights powered by a wind pump perched atop the church tower. And Angells, who it might have been thought would be loath to see his tranquil isolation pass, was, instead, delighted to find himself once more relaxed, contented, happy, and very much in love. True, he later added Phil and Raith to his portfolio, but Ross was always special. Ross was the one who'd made things possible. Ross was the one he cared about most.

"Sir! Sir!"

Topley was wondering if the inspector had fallen asleep with his eyes open.

"Sorry, Sally. Miles away. You finished?"

She nodded. "Back to work?"

"Back to work."

* * *

Ross

OK, the grave. People are more curious about the grave than about the nature of the foursome.

"Doesn't it bother you, sharing your partner with a dead man?"

No, it doesn't, because I'm not. He doesn't love him, not now. It isn't macabre in any way. He doesn't want the grave dug up so that when he dies, their bones can be intertwined for eternity. If it still makes him sad, it's because he's sad at the thought of a life cut short, a glitch in the natural order of things, possibilities never realised. Those thoughts upset him, and also, he's loyal. Loyalty's at the bottom of it. First love. It's always special, isn't it? And you never forget. So if he wants to spend an hour every week tidying up the graveyard, that's fine by me. If he finds it a solace to talk to dead bones in the vicious, evil world he inhabits as part of his job, then that's fine too. I'd rather he did that than downed bottles of whisky to ease his woes. He can't always talk to me, for the obvious reason that some things have to be confidential and he's a good cop and he knows that. I'm really not bothered by the grave. Really.

"Loyalty! You talk about loyalty. He's three-timing you! Four-timing you if you count the dead man in the churchyard!"

Phil, and now Raith, too. Mike's not being disloyal to me. He loves me just as much as he always has, and if I'm not jealous of two very much alive, successful men, I'm not going to be jealous of one very dead one, am I? I can assure you, if he gets wet dreams and wakes me up in the middle of the night with a hard-on, it's not because he's dreaming of Sam Mitford. A dead man's bones are hardly going to push me out of bed, are they? I'm pretty grounded in reality, and the reality is that I don't feel myself threatened—neither by the living nor the dead. There are no bloody ghosts.

I've had that sort of conversation countless times. How wrong I was. The dead do come back to haunt you.

Chapter 9

Angells was back in his office, trawling through information relating to the case he'd been working on with Topley, when a call came through for him.

"It's Falconer on the phone," he was told. "Asked for you, sir."

He was surprised to find that it wasn't Thijs Falconer on the line, but David Falconer, a chartered accountant and the suspect's father. David Falconer asked to see him, but he refused to give details over the phone. So Angells collected Bingham, one of the DCs, in the CID room, and in the constable's car they drove to the Falconers' address on the outskirts of town.

Large, detached, 1930s-style bungalow, garage, large, neat garden bounded by fences and a wall, and a house name as well as a number—'Valkenier'. *Some French word maybe?* Angells wondered as he rang the bell.

David Falconer opened the door and, at his request, Angells entered the living room alone. The son was nowhere to be seen.

David Falconer got straight to the point of the visit.

"If I were you, Inspector," he said, "I wouldn't try to implicate my son in John Coverham's death."

So that's it, thought Angells. *Somehow the son's sussed I'm gay and they think they can put the black on me. I'll have them both banged up.*

Angells turned to the door to call DC Bingham. He intended to issue a warning, but Falconer stopped him mid-action by saying, "Ask your partner, Whitburn, about Gert Schleppers."

"What? Who?" asked Angells in surprise. "How do you know the name of my partner?"

"Gert Schleppers, Inspector," said David Falconer, meeting Angells' puzzled gaze with a slightly mocking smile and ignoring Angells' request about Ross. "Go home. Ask him about Gert Schleppers, and then come back and see me. Without your little colleague there. On your own."

The two men looked at each other. Angells dropped his gaze first.

* * *

"He comes out of that room like a bloody whirlwind," said Bingham, later. "Pushes me out of the front door and says 'Drive!' Well, I don't have bloody ESP, do I? So I says, 'Where to, sir?' and he says, 'The bloody station. Fast!' And he don't say nuthin' else but 'faster' till we get here. He's out of the car before I've even stopped it, and I'm five minutes sat there shakin' like a jelly cos I've just narrowly missed one cyclist, two old ladies, three schoolkids, a tree, six cars and a head-on collision with a double-decker bus."

"He leaps over security," added PC Hope, whose job it was that day to check staff in and out.

"Then he's through the door there." DC Hanrish took up the story. "Doin' a Colin Jackson over the desks and knockin' my stuff all over the floor to boot. Then he races into his room, and a minute later, he's racin' back out, zippin' up his leathers as he goes."

"Then he nearly knocks Lynne Drake an' me

down in the car park," added another, "cos he's already doin' a ton on that machine of his."

"Then the barrier's closing after my car," put in PC Parry, "and he lays the bike sideways and he just scrapes under the bar. Bloody brilliant piece of manoeuvring, even if it did scare us shitless. One of the traffic boys said he clocked him doing 120 heading west."

"Then," said Hanrish again, "the super, he comes out of his office and says, 'Was that Inspector Angells?' all bewildered like, and we say, 'Yes, sir, but he's gone out again,' cos we can't say, 'No, sir, it was a bloody madman!' can we?"

* * *

Ross was in the storehouse talking to one of the BOTWAC residents when, to his surprise, partly because he knew that Angells was on lates and partly because Angells always rode the final few hundred metres slowly, he heard the bike roar to a stop outside.

"You're home nice and early," he began to say, but he was harshly interrupted.

"I want to see you. Now," said Angells roughly.

"Pardon?" said Ross in protest. "I'm sorting something out here."

"Then sort it later. Don't bloody fuss. Get home. Now!"

It suddenly occurred to the curator that the man standing in front of him was not the one who would whisper sweet nothings into his ear at night. It was the man who spent the greater part of his waking hours dealing with those who inhabited much seedier environs. Angells looked formidable.

"I'll be straight along," Ross said, capitulating

sensibly. Angells turned on his heels and left without another word.

He was seated at their little kitchen table. Everything around him was just as it had been when he'd left for work that morning: oranges and apples in a glass bowl on the dresser, jugs of fresh flowers on the window sills, washed breakfast dishes standing on the drainer by the sink.

Angells inhaled deeply, as though to breathe in and capture, forever, normality in his lungs, then he felt his stomach muscles tighten. What was he going to hear?

Ross felt Angells' eyes follow him as he too sat down. At least he seemed less aggressive and belligerent than he had been five minutes earlier, but it was hard to know what was going on behind his 'policeman' face.

So this was how it felt to be in an interview room. Given that the men were seated opposite each other, the scene had all the feeling of an interrogation.

"Who is Gert Schleppers?"

Ross's mouth fell open in astonishment. He stared at Angells, unwilling to believe he'd heard the name.

"Well?"

"Gert? How do you know—?"

"Never mind how I know. Just tell me. Who is he?"

"Oh jeez. Not 'is'. Was. Oh, Mike, was," Ross said quietly.

He waited for another question. None came, and he found that, although he didn't wish to, he was filling the silence by telling Angells about events that he'd thought—he'd hoped—he'd never have to speak about again.

"As you know," he began tentatively, "I used to

live in the Netherlands. As you know, I always loved the Dutch masters and, after I graduated, I was lucky enough to work at a gallery in Amsterdam for three years. At that time, Amsterdam was probably the place to be for a gay man. In Europe, anyway. There were dozens of gay bars, whole streets whose residents were gay, but you already know all that. And you also know that I shared a house along with a couple of others, and that we had steady partners. I mean, I've told you all that. My partner was Gert Schleppers. One night… one night, Gert died in my arms while I was having sex with him."

"Oh my God," whispered Angells. "How awful. What happened? What was wrong with him? And what's the procedure in Holland? Was there an inquest? What did they do?"

Ross was very quiet.

"There was no inquest, Mike. There was no anything. One of the other guys in the house, his elder brother was a doctor. He signed the death certificate to say that Gert had died of SADS. You've heard of it?"

"Yes, of course I have. Sudden death syndrome, but why the secrecy? I don't see why you… Were there drugs involved?"

"No."

"Then why? Oh, Jesus, Ross. How old was he?"

"Fifteen."

"Oh sweet Jesus," said Angells as he realised where Ross's admission was leading. "You were fuckin' a child. You killed a child."

"I didn't kill him."

"Of course you did!"

"Mike, I didn't," argued Ross. "And he didn't seem like a child."

"Grow up fast in Holland, do they?" Angells

said sarcastically. "How could you? Ah, Jesus. You fuckin' shiter!"

"Listen to me. Please listen. Please!"

"I don't have much choice, do I?" shouted Angells angrily. "And I don't know how you got away with it. I mean, this was Holland, not some godforsaken country where life's so cheap no one cares a fuck. Did you know he was fifteen? At first?"

"No!" insisted Ross. "Of course I didn't! I swear to you, Mike, he was in no way like a child. It was like being with a young man, not like being with a child. I have no desire, I have *never* had a desire, to fondle a child, nor even to look at a photograph of a naked child, and certainly I've never had a desire to have sex with a child. Surely you know that. Please say you believe me."

"I do," said Mike after a pause. "Of course I do. I mean, I know you wouldn't do anythin' like that, but it wouldn't hold up in a courtroom, would it? It's the age on the birth certificate that counts. You know that, but of course you did. That was why it was all clammed up. How? Where does David Falconer come in to this? Did you know him in Holland?"

"David Falconer? Not that I recall, no, but I thought your suspect was called Thijs Falconer. You were talking to Flaxby about him on your mobile. I wasn't listening in. It's hard not to overhear."

"David's the father," said Angells, the eavesdropping being an irrelevancy. "Where does he fit into all this? Tell me what else happened. How did you get away with it?"

"I'd rather you didn't say 'Get away with it'," said Ross defensively. "The implication is that—"

"It's not an implication. Let's not beat about the

bush. You got away with it. Till now, anyway."

Ross lowered his eyes and continued. "Gert was illegitimate, and he didn't know anything about his dad. His mother died when he was ten and he knew that she had died suddenly from some form of cardiac arrest. They lived in Utrecht and—"

"Utrecht?"

"Yes. That's what I said, didn't I?"

"You get sarky with me and I'll bloody thump you. I mean it."

"I'm sorry. I wasn't… I'm just… I wasn't expecting this, and…" Ross took a deep breath. "Gert was sent to an orphanage in Utrecht. Well, you know what can happen to unprotected kids in care. So he ran off to Amsterdam, and when I met him he was selling himself. I looked after him and, in return—"

"You looked after him all right. I've not heard it called that before."

"Oh for goodness' sake! He was promiscuous. If I hadn't taken him in, he'd have probably died of AIDS."

"You did him a favour then, did you? I think not!"

"You know exactly what I mean. And I should have thought that you of all people would know that real and apparent age can be different."

"Meaning what?"

"Meaning that being underage obviously didn't stop you and Sam Mi—"

He didn't get to complete his insult. Angells hit him so hard he fell sideways off the chair.

They rarely argued. They had never resorted to blows.

"I'm sorry," Ross said, wiping his lip. "That's the crassest thing I've ever said to anyone. I can't believe I said it to you."

They stared at each other, dismayed, embarrassed.

"I'm sorry I thumped you," said Angells apologetically.

He held out his hand and helped Ross back onto the chair. Ross paused and then, continuing in a more measured tone, explained.

"So, we—that is, my friend, his brother, myself and a couple of others—we were able to have everything hushed up because we were able to bring pressure to bear on the orphanage management. They accepted that the cause of death was SADS. It transpires that there can be a genetic component to susceptibility, a particular version known as LQTS, and as you doubtless know already, excitement and heightened emotion can trigger a fatal SADS attack. It could have happened at any time—watching a football match, running for a bus, anything. We weren't asking them to lie about the cause of death. Just about the context in which death occurred."

"But David Falconer must know about the context, Ross," said Angells, the reference to Sam Mitford causing his own mood to soften. "He must know that this Gert Scleppers was only fifteen when he died, and that you were fuckin' him and that it was all hushed up."

Angells frowned as he searched for the connection that might link Ross and the Falconers together.

"The Falconers lived in Utrecht. The mam died years ago, but I know that she worked in some sort of care home. I guess it was the orphanage. I'm not for one minute sayin' that she was involved in all this abuse you say was goin' on, but staff talk. If she talked to her husband about stuff, about Gert Schleppers, mentioned your name—I mean, it's not unusual, but he's from Sunderland. He'd know Whitburn, wouldn't he? The place, that is. It'd stick. Make a link. Maybe for years he's thought nuthin' of it. Then this happens and the son mentions me. I know it's a small world, but how would the dad know of you here? Of us?"

"I don't know. Perhaps he's been to the gallery or seen my name on a catalogue. There's always a bit of a bio. Three years in the Netherlands, et cetera. As you said, it could ring a bell, and there are dozens of people who know about us."

"Mm. He works for Ormerley FC. He realises he can use what he knows to his advantage. You've spent the last five years or more livin' within shoutin' distance of a man who can bang you up in a Dutch jail for... all manner of things. Sex with a minor, withholdin' information, pervertin' the course of justice, manslaughter possibly. You name it. He can do it."

Interpreting Angells' expression at that moment would have proved an easy feat for even the most insensitive of souls: sheer misery.

"Ross, you should have told me," he said despairingly. "Raith, Phil—do they know? Have you told them?"

"No! It was *past*. It wasn't *now*. I wanted to forget it. Are you saying I should tell them?"

"You *can't* tell them. You'd implicate them in the crime. Tar them with the same fuckin' brush you've just tarred me with. Ah, shite! You should have told me!" he repeated.

"Oh yes? How so? As in, 'Oh, by the way, a kid died when I shot him full of semen, but don't worry, it was all neatly hushed up so we'll just move on.' Could you have just moved on? Then? Now?" he asked almost inaudibly. He was fearful of the answer. None arrived, which was almost worse. "Look, no one was wrongfully imprisoned because of this. There were no family members deprived of justice for their dead relation."

"That makes it all right, does it? You think so?" said Angells, his anger returning. "No, it bloody well doesn't. Not even if it had had nuthin' to do with the bloody Falconers. You know what he's goin' to want from me, don't you? Take the heat off his son—somehow—and that means lettin' everyone chase round huntin' for some other collar to finger. Waste everyone's time. Pretend I don't know. Deceive everyone. The super, all the boys and girls there. Be a bigger shit than you for what you did. I'd never be able to look any of them in the eye again. I'd be too ashamed. And that assumes I'd get away with it. If I got found out, we'd both get sent down. A bent cop in jail, a bent gay cop in jail." An image of the treatment he'd receive flashed through his mind, and he felt his pulse quicken with panic. "God, Ross, the thought of what they'd do to me!"

For a full five minutes, Angells sat there, his eyes closed, his head in his hands. Then, abruptly, he stood up, strode out and rode off. Ross had no idea when, indeed if, he'd be back.

* * *

Angells felt the need to get away from Ross, away from Tunhead, and, on his own, consider what he'd learnt and what he'd do. There was a small layby close to the junction of the country road that followed Tun Beck north and the trunk road that led east to Warbridge and on to the coast. He pulled into it and killed the engine. In front of him, the road to his job. Behind him, the road to his home of the last ten years. Which was more important? Tunhead or Warbridge? Where did his loyalties lie?

Think, he told himself. *For God's sake, think. Calmly. Logically. Think! Give yourself one good reason why you should tell David Falconer to go and fuck himself.* The answer came immediately: *your job. You love your job and you're good at it. Love it despite that shithole, Fortune. In the super, you've a friend, not just a colleague. He trusts in your judgement and ability. You enjoy your responsibilities. You pride yourself on discharging your duties well. You enjoy the thrill of the chase. You get satisfaction from tying up a case and seeing some shiter you've been after put where they can't do harm. Your job gives you self-respect and self-confidence. In a sense, it defines you. So you can't do what the Falconers want. Cos if you did, you'd have to give up your job. You couldn't stay.*

Such awareness was crystal clear. If Angells did what the Falconers wanted, he'd have to resign. He'd never be able to look Flaxby in the eye again. He wouldn't be able to face anybody at the station and tell them how to do their work—not if he was as bent and contemptible as the scum they spent their lives catching. He'd be worse than scum. Beneath contempt in their eyes if they knew. Beyond despicable in his own.

"I can't do what they want," he said aloud. "I can't do it. Every fuckin' bit of logic and common sense tells me I can't—and every bit of me that isn't logic and isn't common sense tells me that I have to!"

For behind him, back along the valley road, was the one place in which he felt true happiness. Moors for wandering and rambling over, pretty little gorges for slithering and scrambling through.

A cosy house to spend a peaceful evening in. Perhaps not quite so peaceful when Raith appeared, though equally pleasurable, equally satisfying. Phil's frequent visits, when the four of them would sit and talk, and under Phil's calming spell, relax, and feel at peace with each other and with the world.

Tunhead was the centre of this world. Mike's first love lay there. His second was there too, very much alive, thank God. For, in the centre's very heart was Ross. There was no one he cared about more. He loved snuggling up to him at night and feeling wanted and cared for. Loved, and was grateful for, Ross's little kindnesses and his willingness to compromise and make allowances. Phil, Raith, the bones in the churchyard… He realised he wasn't the easiest man in the world to live with. And then there were the delights of making love.

Angells was not someone who felt that sex should inevitably end in penetration, but when it did… Prior to knowing Ross, he had always, in the Chief Inspector's words, been the one who topped. Ross, though, in the interests of democracy, and probably self-preservation, had asked if they could sometimes switch roles. Angells had been surprised and bemused to realize that, although the role he preferred was the one he'd always had, the 'moment' most certainly wasn't. When 10ccs of what had been inside Ross pounded into him instead, he felt an intimacy which was painfully sweet. And on the occasions when he managed to time his own climax to match his partner's, he felt as though the pair of them had melted into one another. The sensation overwhelmed him so much that his eyes would glisten with tears.

But what if he were caught? He'd made a lot of enemies in his time on the Force. Old collars would be committing crimes just to get their hands on him. Queueing up. He retched and swallowed hard to keep down vomit begotten by fear.

"Oh, Jesus," he moaned as images of rape and torture passed one after the other behind his closed lids like a horrifying slide show. He opened his eyes to force himself to look at the road, the bike, anything but the pictures in his head, but it didn't help. They were still there.

If he got sent down, there'd only be one way out and that was to hang himself in his prison cell, but would he manage to do so before the gloating inmates got to him?

"And even if I don't get caught," he said aloud, "if I leave…" He knew the badge protected him. It kept him safe—relatively so, at any rate. Without its protection, he'd be fair game for any folk who fancied their chances of settling old scores.

He could avoid all the fear and the promise of pain. He could keep the job he loved. He just had to refuse to play Falconer's ball. He was tempted.

He kicked the bike into action, aware that he was heading into danger. Three things hung in the balance. He'd fight to keep one but, in doing so, he knew he'd lose the second, and—God help him—he knew he could lose the third. Well, he'd have to risk it. He knew where his loyalty lay.

So he turned left at the junction and rode back to Warbridge and the Falconers' house where, this time, both father and son were waiting. He told them he would fix it.

He was halfway down the drive when Thijs Falconer chased after him.

"Mr Angells," he shouted. When he got close, he asked, "Please, please could you go into

John's and get some videos for me? He liked to film us doing things."

"Is this some kind of joke?" asked the DI in disbelief. "Do you know what the max is for misconduct in office? Life! Not that I'd last out for long by the time I'd got raped to rags and beaten to pulp. And you're not content with that? You want me to go and get some videos too. What else would you like? A coke and bloody popcorn?" he asked sarcastically.

"Inspector, please. If you saw them you'd understand."

"I don't need to understand. I already understand. You and your father should go back to whatever sewer you crawled out of. You've got what you want from me. You don't need nuthin' else."

"Please—"

"Fuck off, man!" yelled Angells as Thijs Falconer grabbed his arm and tried to stop him turning his bike around.

"Please, Inspector. Please. Please get them. Look at them if you want. You'll understand then."

There was such desperation in the young man's face that Angells stopped pulling his arm away.

"Forensics will have been through the place with a fine-toothed comb," he said less belligerently. "No one's turned up any videos."

"That's because they were hidden, and they probably weren't looking. I know where they are, but I can't get them, can I? I can't go there. You could, though. Please. I don't want Dad to see them. I don't want anyone to see them. Unless you look. If you have to."

"Jesus Christ. This gets worse," said Angells. "Go on then. What am I lookin' for?"

And, sitting at home next evening, having played the videos through, he could see why Thijs Falconer so desperately wanted them recovered and kept safe. Ross had once jokingly asked his lover if he'd joined the police force so he could experiment with confiscated property in the safety of his bedroom and watch hard porn officially.

"I'll leave the handcuffs and everything else at the station," Angells had answered, "and most of the porn has little or no effect."

Though how would he describe how what he was looking at now was affecting him? It wasn't all the B and D that Falconer and Coverham had indulged in. That was nasty. Dangerous. But not sickening. He'd seen much worse without the tiniest flicker of emotion. The other stuff though… How, in God's name, could a dad do such awful things to his son?

"Sir," said DC Topley, two days later, "the Coverham case. We have to pull Thijs Falconer in again. He lied to us."

Angells felt his pulse quicken, but it returned to its normal slow, steady beat as he realised that the recall was nothing to do with any new evidence, other than the fact that Falconer had lied about how he'd got home on the day of the footballer's death.

"He said he'd got the bus from Raneleigh Street. He couldn't have. I was talking to a friend in Traffic, and she was saying how relieved they all were that things were back to normal now. Apparently, the road's been up for days and the 145s were all re-routed. So if Falconer lied about that, and we know the taxis haven't come up with anything, maybe he got a lift and said something about what happened to whoever was driving. Possible, isn't it?"

Angells forced himself to sound congratulatory.

"Good work, Sally," he said. "I'll contact him and drive over, and we can interview him together if you want."

"I'll drive out and get him if it's easier, sir."

"No, it's fine," said Angells, knowing he'd need to talk to Falconer first. "He knows me from the other day. I'll sort it."

* * *

"That's why my dad got on to you," the young man explained as Angells drove the two of them back to the station a little later. "He knew I'd messed up over the buses, and he said that if you thought I'd lied about that one thing, then I might have lied about others. Then you'd keep on at me till I admitted I pushed him. Pushed John."

Angells said nothing. That was exactly what Topley had thought.

"You've... We've got to deal with this. So your dad collected you," Angells said, repeating what Falconer had told him. "You'll have to say you didn't tell him what had gone on at Manny's."

"I didn't tell him then. I only told him later. So that's true."

Angells just pulled a face as if to say "glad something is."

"Why make up that story about the bus then? Why didn't you just say your dad had picked you up? You've made stuff complicated."

"Because... Did you get my videos, Mr Angells?" Falconer asked nervously. "Were you able to?"

"Yes."

"Did you watch them?"

"Some."

"Did you watch the one John and me set up in my house without my dad knowing?"

"Yes."

"Well you'll know I couldn't tell him, could I? Not straight away. I had to tell him, obviously, but I was calmer then and I could stand up to him a bit. Even so, he..." The young man stopped talking and stared through the car window without really seeing any of the traffic.

Angells pulled over.

"OK, man. Look. I know your dad's a shiter who's been abusin' you for years. And I know you're scared of him, but you can't say that when we get to the station. Cos if you bring your dad into this, then he's on an abuse charge—which he fuckin' deserves—but you're still facin' a possible manslaughter, and God only knows what charges my partner and I are facin'."

Falconer nodded. "So what shall I say?"

Jesus, thought Angells. *I'm workin' out what lies a suspect should say. Christ! What would pull the wool over Topley's eyes? Nuthin'.* She was far too smart.

"The less *you* say the better," he decided. "Just keep sayin' you don't know why you lied. It's weak, but I'll make sure I ask the questions, and I won't keep pushin' for answers."

"Thank you, Inspector."

"Piss off," Angells said angrily. "You think I'm doin' this for you?"

He restarted the car and silently drove to the station.

* * *

Phil

All four of us have a small tattoo, a blue infinity symbol across a red heart. Hence the tattoo is known as the infinity heart, and it has become a symbol of polyamory. Even Ross has one, and he isn't entirely certain he's poly. (He is, of course.) Ross, Mike and I have our tattoo on our upper arm. Raith's is on his neck. It's the only tattoo that Ross and I have. Skin is just another canvas to Raith, and he has several. Mike just has two, the infinity heart on his arm and a stunning tattoo on his back which Raith designed for him.

Our infinity hearts are in outline, not blocks of colour. The blue represents honesty and openness. The red represents love and passion. I think of them as little badges. Badges of loyalty, forever tattooed on our arms.

We're not promiscuous. Personally, I can't imagine going outside our quad, and I'm sure that's true of the others too. Perhaps it's foolish to trust other people to that extent: we're human after all; but we're supportive of each other and I believe that we satisfy each other. It would take something extreme to cause one of us to lapse. I'm confident of that, and because of that confidence, I know that there'd be no ranting recriminations, only concern and a comforting arm. But I can't see it happening.

The relationships aren't necessarily sexual. Ross and I have never had intercourse with each other, but we care about each other's happiness in a far deeper way than we might care about that of our other friends. We share as much as we can, financially, legally... Ross and Mike are partners officially, so, for example, they'd inherit each other's worldly goods should anything happen to one of them. (Heaven forbid!) However, we decided we'd all draw up wills. Apart from some specific bequests, all our assets are now shared. Not that they would mean much without the person who bequeathed them.

As far as I know, none of us are hiding deep or damaging secrets. The problem with secrets is their definition: they are secret.

Chapter 10

Some nights, sleep simply doesn't come. Angells was having one of those nights. Thijs Falconer's videos were lying on the kitchen table, ready to be returned to him the following morning on Angells' way to work. The last time he would take that road to work. He had holidays owing. He'd take them in lieu of working his notice.

He lay in bed and, through a gap in the curtains, watched the swaying boughs of the tree across the road from the little house. Trees struggled to gain a foothold in this windblown part of the country. There was only the one. Had Angells had a poetic rather than pragmatic turn of mind, he might have seen in nature a desolation to mirror his feelings.

He'd always had good night vision once his eyes adjusted to the darkness. He wouldn't need it anymore. He wouldn't have to spend any more nights sitting in a cold car or in an unfamiliar room waiting for an informer's tip-off to deliver some action. He could spend his nights cosily in Tunhead, tucked up with one of his lovers. Was that a comfort? *It ought to be*, he thought.

Of course, Flaxby would want to know why he was resigning. He couldn't tell him the truth. He'd say what the super had sensed already—that his mind wasn't wholly on the job and he therefore felt it was best to leave before he compromised the workings of the division. But he knew that if this hadn't happened, he'd have worked out the problem of divided loyalties. If he hadn't felt so cornered, he'd have found a means of reconciling his love of his job with his love of Tunhead and the people there. All hypothetical now. Why even give it consideration?

There were financial implications. He lay there totting up the sums. Ross was certain they'd manage—until he found another job, that was—but perhaps Ross was just saying so to make him feel less stressed. He was far too young to take early retirement.

He realised he was scared of being just a member of the public. He wouldn't have the job to... to what? Hide behind? Yes, in a way. He knew it was counterintuitive, but the job helped to keep him safe. What's more, it made him brave. Not foolhardy, but brave. He lived with the knowledge that he was a cop, that he had a certain standing and authority, that he'd tolerate no nonsense.

Nothing would change on the outside, but everything would change within. *It's like wearin' armour,* he thought. *I've been walkin' down the street wearin' armour and, now, I'll feel naked. Naked and vulnerable.* He didn't seek out trouble but, off-duty, he still wore the invisible armour and, armed with the ID he always carried with him, would wade in to sort a dispute out. Now, he'd be one of those who cross the street and look the other way.

Jeez, he thought, *even bein' brave's a sham. What other wonderful things am I goin' t' learn about myself before this mess is finished?*

Ross stirred slightly in his sleep beside him.

"You bloody nuisance," Angells said softly, and finally, fitfully, he slept.

The sound of the bedside alarm woke him far too quickly. He slowly eased himself out of bed, washed and shaved, and went downstairs. He couldn't stomach a breakfast—not today—but he made himself a cup of coffee. He heard the floorboards creak.

"Last day, Ross," said Angells as Ross made an equally early appearance in their kitchen.

"Mike, I am so sorry."

Angells shrugged.

"Me too, but, well, there's no other way."

He gathered his belongings together.

"Not sure what time I'll be back. I'll need to talk to the super. I'll drop the videos off at Thijs Falconer's on my way in."

"Be careful, Mike," pleaded Ross as Angells opened the door.

"What?" Angells' mind was already on other things and he wasn't really listening.

"Be careful, please. That's all."

Angells gave a wry smile. "Don't worry. I want to talk to him about what happened, but I know I'm not a social worker. Just a cop. For one more day, anyhow. Maybe I can help a bit, though."

"I don't doubt that's your intention, love, and it deserves a medal, but you might find yourself treading treacherously deep water."

"Shallow end only. I promise."

A brief goodbye kiss, and he left.

He took his car. This was partly because he didn't wish to draw more attention to himself than was necessary when visiting the Falconers' house: a man in leathers on a loud, powerful bike was likely to make a few curtains twitch, even on a non-estate part of town with houses well back from the road. Also, there were a few items still at work that he knew he'd be bringing home. Last day. What a way for his career to end.

The drive to work took around an hour in the car, the drive home forty-five minutes or less. The implication wasn't lost on him. Nevertheless, he'd never envisaged leaving before his due retirement date. There was no euphoria, just a sense of sadness, loss, regret and more than a little fear.

He took a bend a little sharply. *Careful, Mike*, he warned himself, *else you won't have any choice in the matter.*

Don't have a choice anyway, he reminded himself as reality swerved starkly in.

Angells rang the doorbell. A minute later, Thijs Falconer opened the door.

"Your videos," Angells said, keeping hold of them in his outstretched hand. "I'd like to talk to you about them."

Thijs Falconer nodded and, subdued, led the way into the living room and sat on the edge of the sofa. Angells glanced at the various chairs but chose to sit down next to him. He knew that a tender touch might get him somewhere but a tough one most certainly wouldn't. The lad had had enough of tough.

"Look," said Angells gently, "if you go on like this, you're goin' to end up on a slab in the morgue. I've seen it happen. I know what I'm talkin' about. You're goin' to get a guy who won't stop. You'll be beggin' him to, but he won't. It happens, Thijs."

On purpose, he'd used the lad's first name. Not 'Falconer'.

"I can't do it any other way," said the young man after a pause. "When all that B and D stuff's happening, when it was happening with John, then I could forget about all the other stuff. The stuff that was happening here."

"The stuff with your dad." A statement not a question.

"Mm. It made me forget. The pain made me forget."

How crazy, thought Angells. *Using one pain to mask another.*

"Your dad, how long has it been goin' on?"

"A long time. Ever since Mum died. Perhaps before that. There was nothing I could do. I just had to let him."

"I know, man," said Angells, adding encouragingly, "but you could do something now. You could get a place of your own, find a nice boy."

"Could I? Well, I tried, didn't I?" he said bitterly. "I begged and begged John to come out about us. I wanted to move in with him, like you and your Ross. Be out. Go places together. Let everyone know we were a couple. But he wouldn't, would he? He didn't love me enough to do it. If he loved me, he should have come out, shouldn't he?"

Angells pulled a face. He wondered what else Falconer might know about his life in Tunhead.

"It's not always as easy as you're makin' it out to be, Thijs," said Angells with understanding. "He was a soccer player. How many soccer players do you know who've said they're gay? They're not goin' to, are they? The showers, the big bath, even the hugs when you put the ball in the net, and the stick from the terraces! It's not so easy. God, I should know."

"How do you mean—you should know? You're out."

"Yes, I am, and thank God, I've never had to be otherwise. But I know how it used to be in the

Force. Not so long ago either, and if I'd been gay then I might've kept it a secret just like your John did. In fact, I'd've probably had to. That or lose my job."

The young man looked surprised.

"Why would you have lost your job?"

"Because they'd've thought me a security risk and pressured me into resignin'. Not macho enough to take on some axe-slingin' thug so puttin' my colleagues in danger. So I'd probably've kept it quiet, and then I'd've opened myself up to blackmail. Ironic, isn't it? When it isn't my bein' gay that you and your dad are blackmailin' me for."

Falconer said nothing. He had the decency to look embarrassed.

"Even now," Angells continued, "OK, everyone at work knows about me, but I'm not goin' to start bangin' on about gay rights trainin' for coppers or sumthin'. Or put myself forward to provide it. I can see where you're comin' from, truly I can, but I understand where your John was comin' from too."

"I still think that if he'd loved me enough…"

"So, just for the record, what did happen that day?" Angells asked, rather abruptly changing the subject. "I know you've told me some of it before, but put it all together."

"Like I told you at the station, we'd been arguing all night, all morning," said Falconer. "He doesn't… didn't know Warbridge well. He didn't know Manny's Bar, and I thought I'd take him somewhere where it's obvious, make him hold my hand or something."

"That was stupid, man. You were cornerin' him."

"I know that now, don't I? But at the time, it wasn't what I was thinking. When he realised, he was furious. He went storming into the toilets. I went after him and we were still arguing, and then I got angry and I pushed him. I didn't punch him hard or anything, but I suppose he was surprised and he lost his balance. It was an accident. I mean, I didn't expect he'd lose his balance. Perhaps there was water on the floor and he slipped. I don't know."

He took a while to compose himself.

"Well, the first time you interviewed me, at Cinders and then back at the station, you and that other policeman, that was OK. I'd talked to my dad about it and he said just to say that we were arguing and that I'd been upset and run, which was true. Don't mention pushing him or anything. Then, when you realised I'd lied about the way I got home, we thought, if they think there's been one lie they might think there are others. And then I was really scared. Dad said that it wouldn't be murder. It would be manslaughter and that I might get up to five years, but I didn't want to go to jail. It's not a good place for gays, is it? I'd have got AIDS and…"

"That'd be the least of your worries, but go on."

"And anyway, he was thinking of himself too. Dad was. So, it was just luck, him knowing about your Ross—"

"Luck! Luck? It didn't occur to you that if *I* messed up we'd both be banged up, you and I both? And your dad for blackmail. Though the fucker deserves that. And Ross. It didn't bother your consciences that you were putting the black on?"

Thijs looked ashamed. "No," he admitted. "I'm sorry. Would I have got five years?" he asked after a while.

"I doubt it. Be pretty harsh that, given the

circumstances. Maybe suspended. Maybe a short stretch. Still bad for a gay." *Especially one as scared and vulnerable as you,* he thought but didn't say.

"Would you keep the videos, Mr Angells? Destroy them or something. I don't want dad to find them."

"Yeah. I'll take them with me then. Don't worry. They won't be found." *Unless they need to be,* he was thinking. He didn't say he'd already taken copies. An insurance policy should he ever hear from David Falconer again.

"Did *your* dad... did he... did he mess you around?"

"No, thank God. Not at all."

"Does he know you're gay?"

"We never talked about it, but he'd have had to be blind not to know. He died when I was in my teens though."

"I'm sorry. How? What did he die of?"

"Buried under a lorry load of stone when a road caved in. He was a quarryman."

He'd thought the world of his dad, but he could speak about his dad's death with far greater equanimity than he could speak about Sam Mitford's.

"You're a quarryman's son?" said Thijs in wonderment.

"Yes. Why do you sound so surprised?"

"Don't know really. I suppose I thought that that sort of work, the sons always followed in their father's footsteps. Straight into a job in the quarries. Keep outsiders out. You didn't want to do that?"

"There weren't many footsteps to follow and jobs to walk into. Most of the quarries had closed by the time I left school. No future in it."

What the fuck am I doin'? thought Angells. The conversation had turned far too personal. Time to turn it back.

"Look," he said, "regardin' John Coverham, him bein' a soccer player and that, sometimes there's got to be secrets. It might wreck you and make life hell, but the alternative's worse."

Thijs Falconer thought about this for a time, then said, "I wish I hadn't hit him, Inspector Angells. I wish he were still alive. I miss him so much. I even miss the things he did to me."

The young man was fighting back tears now, and Angells did what, to a compassionate man like himself, was the obvious thing to do. Probably the only thing a man like Angells could do. He reached out and, despite Ross's warning ringing shrilly in his ears, placed a comforting arm around the young man's shoulders and held him close. Then, clasp turned to kiss, kiss to kisses, kisses to groping hands, to frantic undressing and intercourse.

They lay in Thijs's bedroom in each other's arms.

"You were wired," Thijs said, no hint of condemnation in his voice. "That's why you wanted me to go over everything again. *For the record...*"

Angells shrugged.

"Well, if it's still running and if it can pick up from the floor, you can play it over and wank or something when you get home."

"I'm sorry. Once a cop..." He let the sentence hang.

"Doesn't matter. You're nice, Inspector Angells," said Thijs with a sad smile. He ran the tips of his fingers over Angells' face. "Do you look like your dad?" he asked.

For an instant, Angells felt annoyed with himself again. He hadn't come here to discuss *his* life or *his* family. He was letting the young man—the suspect in an investigation, no, the self-confessed perpetrator—direct a conversation. Then genuine concern resurfaced and he thought, *If that's what it takes*, and answered.

"I've got his colouring. His eyes."

There was a long silence, broken by Thijs Falconer.

"Thank you for trying to talk to me about stuff, Mr Angells. Would you be able to come and talk to me again? Fuck, too, if you want."

"No," said Angells quietly.

"So, you care, but not that much."

A statement rather than a question, which was just as well, as Angells had no honest answer to offer.

"It's OK, Inspector. Would have been nice, that's all."

"I better go."

"Five more minutes?"

Angells shook his head. This wouldn't do. He knew it wouldn't do. He dressed, watched by the young man who lay still and half-naked on the bed. He bent over to kiss him a final time, but Thijs turned his head away and Angells could see that tears were trickling across his cheek. He kissed him anyway, tasting salt.

"Take care," he said gently. He picked up the videos and left.

* * *

Ron Fortune was at his desk when an internal call came through from Flaxby at *his* desk.

"Ron? My office please. Five minutes."

Not like Flaxby to be so secretive. Wondering what was bugging him, Fortune knocked on the door in two.

"What's up?" he asked, placing papers on the floor and sitting down.

"The Falconer lad," said the super. "The one the DI's been dealing with. He's just been pulled out from under the three thirty-five to Newcastle."

"You're joking!"

"Do I look like I'm bloody joking?"

Fortune's first reaction was relief.

"Shit! At least he wasn't in custody. It didn't happen here," he said.

He knew from past experience how unpleasant life became for everyone when a DSI occurred—a suspect's death or serious injury in or shortly after custody. There was always a thorough, searching investigation, and you could find yourself before the IPCC, the professional standards department, who'd want to check that every government-approved procedure had been scrupulously adhered to. A DSI was something no one wished to have—usually. Fortune's relief was quickly followed by elation. Even if the storm blew quickly over, the damage would leave a question mark against the name of the main investigating officer. One in the eye for Angela!

"So, him not being in custody is going to make a whole lot of difference, is it?" Flaxby was saying. "It's still a DSI matter, and once it's clear the lad was gay and our number one suspect in the Coverham case—"

"But Angells put him out of the frame. He cleared him."

"No matter. We'll have the Gay Rights Brigade screaming police brutality and heavy handedness driving the lad to top himself—"

"But *Angells* is gay—"

"—and all that shit, and we'll have the IPCC crawling all over us, checking that everything was done by the book. At least it was Angells. It would be by the book."

An implication that if he, Fortune, had been in charge, it wouldn't have? The chief inspector wasn't sure. The super knew his feelings about 'them', and no doubt had deduced that Angells' and Fortune's modus operandi would have been considerably different.

"We need to get everyone in first thing tomorrow. I don't care if they're going to their own funeral. They postpone it and get in here. Can you sort that, Ron? I need to talk to Mike, Topley and Sanghera. Are they in?"

"Angells and Sanghera are. Topley, no."

"Well, I want to know exactly what they did and what they said. I want to know how much goddamn breath they took when they said it. And I want to know it all before word gets upstairs to Mayfield. I'll start with Mike, and I'll need the interview tapes too. I'll take them home. Mother of Mercies, I hate this sort of thing."

Fortune would have commiserated if it wasn't for the fact that he half hoped the super's sodding Angela had put at least a big toe wrong.

* * *

Angells had just printed the resignation letter he had typed some days before. He hadn't wasted any time. He'd gone straight to the station after talking to the Falconers and typed the letter before he'd even changed out of his leathers. Now, he dated it and signed it and, with a heavy heart, reached for an envelope. He didn't have one and so, with the letter in his hand, he was on his way to the stationery cupboard when the super stopped him.

"We've got some trouble, Mike," said Flaxby quietly. "My office. Come on."

"Thijs Falconer," said Flaxby as soon as they'd shut the door. "Threw himself under a train an hour past."

He was halfway through saying that remains were being collected and taken to the morgue, when the inspector wheeled round, grabbed the nearby filing cabinet for support and vomited onto the piece of paper he was carrying.

"Use the bloody bucket, Mike!" shouted Flaxby. "Don't just stand there. Here!" He handed his wastepaper basket over. "Bloody hell!"

Gradually, vomiting changed to retching and then to some composure, albeit with the cabinet as a form of crutch.

"I'm sorry, sir," said Angells, wiping sick off his mouth with his shirt sleeve and dropping the wet letter into the bucket but offering no explanation.

"Are you all right?" Flaxby was genuinely concerned.

Angells nodded. "Yes, sir," he said, repeating an apology.

"Shock, was it?" The super was observing him carefully.

"Yes, sir. Or sumthin' I've eaten."

"OK. Wipe that crap off yourself and clean up my filing cabinet. I'll be in the chief inspector's room, seeing as you've turned mine into Warbridge High Street on a Saturday night. And throw out the bloody bucket too."

It wasn't something he'd eaten that had made Angells vomit. Nor was it shock. Flaxby knew that. He knew what had caused it too—the two fingers his inspector had shoved down his throat when he'd turned away. He'd made sure that vomit had covered whatever he'd been holding. *What the hell was on that sheet of paper?* Flaxby wondered.

Angells didn't know if he could trust his legs to hold him up, so he leant against the cabinet, forcing himself to inhale and exhale deeply and slowly. When he was sure he could stand unaided, he placed the bucket on the top of the cabinet and took off his shirt. Then, with the bucket in one hand and his shirt in the other, he went through the CID room, down the corridor and into the toilets. Rolled eyes followed him, but he was aware of none of them. He kept his eyes on the ground in front of him, wondering how he was going to deal with the fallout from what he'd just been told. From a personal point of view. From a professional point of view. He hadn't foreseen this. No way had he foreseen it.

Almost on autopilot, he flushed the contents of the bucket down the toilet bowl, washed the sleeve of his shirt in a sink and wrung it out, washed his face and, as best he could, gargled till the smell of vomit faded. More collected now, he flushed the bowl once again, just to make certain that no paper had stuck in the u-bend, put his wet shirt back on, discarded the bucket, cleaned Flaxby's office furniture and room as best he could, then, leaden legged, went to Fortune's office as instructed.

By the time Angells returned, DC Sanghera was already in the DCI's room telling Flaxby and Fortune what had happened at Cinderella's and then afterwards at the station.

"Nothing was amiss, sir. Sirs," he said, looking from one to the other and attempting to address them both. "There was no undue pressure. Nothing."

"OK, Sunny," said Flaxby, certain that the young constable was being truthful.

"Will it go down, you know… promotion prospects? Bein' involved in an inquiry. Mud sticks, doesn't it?"

"As far as I can see, there's no mud. Not on you," said Flaxby. "Poor lad," he said, after the young man had returned to the CID room. "He's not going to know what's hit him if the questions start. We'll make it as easy as possible for him. For Sally Topley too."

Angells knocked at the door.

Flaxby thought about the fingers down the throat. "Not sure about this one, though," he said, to Fortune's puzzlement, as Angells entered the room.

"Now," said Flaxby, in a more menacing voice than the one he'd used with Sanghera. "Sit down. Everything. From start to finish. Every second. Every nanosecond. Cinders. The interview with you and Sunny Sanghera. The interview with you and Sally Topley, and why you let your main, your *only*, suspect walk out of here and under a train."

The sole difference between Angells' and Sanghera's accounts of the visit to Cinderella's and the subsequent interview was that, despite feeling that the strings holding him in place were snapping, Angells gave his in his customary clear reporting style.

"And the second interview? With Topley?" asked Flaxby.

Just then, Fortune's phone rang, saving Angells from thinking of an answer that would minimise the damage. He knew he hadn't exactly pressed hard when he'd had Thijs Falconer in the second time. Indeed, he'd made a point of deflecting Topley's pressure.

"It's the chief," said Fortune to Flaxby. "She's heard. She wants to see you."

"Shit. What time are you in tomorrow?" Flaxby asked Angells gruffly.

"Ten, sir."

"Make it nine. We need to sort this out. And look as normal as you can for a while. Use your car, not your bike, and leave your leathers in Tunhead. I'm serious. Understood?"

Angells nodded. "Yes, sir," he said contritely.

The super left. Fortune and Angells looked at each other, Angells' face full of concern, Fortune's almost gloating.

"He's worried, Angela. Should he be?" Fortune asked complacently. It wasn't *him* in the hot seat.

Angells met his superior's stare with one of his own. *You'd like that, wouldn't you?* he thought. *Well, sod you, I'm not givin' you the pleasure of an answer.*

"Do you know if there's a suicide note?" he asked. God knows what would be in one if there were.

"Too early to know."

"Anything else? Can I go now?"

"Home? You still feel sick?"

"No. Just back to what I was doin'. To work." For Angells had realised that, far from handing in his notice, he would have to stay. If he left now, it would look too suspicious, and anyway, there was unfinished business to attend to. The details were fuzzy and none too clear. Yet.

He returned to his own little office, and then the shock did hit him. He was still sitting there, unable to focus on anything other than the events of the past three hours, when the super walked into the room. Before he could say anything, Angells looked at him and spoke with a vehemence that took Flaxby by surprise.

"Life's a shit isn't it?" Angells said. "A bloody awful shit! He was just a lad, Clive. Twenty-bloody-three. What kind of a fuckin' world is it where the only future you think you've got is so bleak that you jump in front of an express train? What's in your head the second before you jump? What blackness? Hopelessness? And what do we do to help? Even when we can, we don't. Not even for five bloody minutes. Five bloody minutes! I'm so fuckin' fed up of men dyin' on me! So fuckin' fed up of it! First one and then another!" He closed his eyes and sighed, Flaxby staring at him, concerned. "I'm sorry," Angells said, as normal service resumed as abruptly as it had been interrupted. "It's just—oh, I dunno."

"Go home." Flaxby's tone was kinder than when they'd spoken earlier. "Nine tomorrow, but go home now. Go on. Anyway, I need your room. Mine stinks. Go on before I change my mind and tell you to swap for the rest of the day."

"You sure, sir?"

"Go on."

"Thank you."

* * *

In his house that evening, Flaxby was discussing some of the day's events with his wife of thirty years.

"I'm his detective superintendent and I never realised," he said. "He's got eyes that don't know whether to be grey or green. A nightmare for a photofit."

"I know," she said. "Very unusual. In eyes. Did you use to play with ollies?"

"Of course. Big bag of them."

"Well some of them had streaks that colour, didn't they? Start off greyish and then change to green. What made you notice them now after all this time?"

"I couldn't not notice really. He'd been crying."

* * *

In *his* house, Ross was waiting at the open door. He'd been listening for the car.

"Thanks for the text," he said gravely as he gave Angells his usual welcome home hug. "You didn't hand your notice in then?"

Angells shook his head. He looked very, very weary. "How could I, Ross? I thought it was finished, but it isn't finished, is it?"

He sat down at their little kitchen table and put his head in his hands. Ross bustled around and set a mug of frothy coffee in front of him. Other than saying, "Thank you," Angells drank it without speaking.

"Do you want to talk about it, love?" asked Ross gently.

"I don't even want to think about it. I don't think I *can* think about it, not tonight anyway. Tomorrow maybe."

"I haven't eaten yet. Would you like something?"

"Dunno. I spewed up my dinner. Sorry if I stink a bit."

"Look," said Ross encouragingly, "why don't you finish that drink then go up and take a shower. Better still, go and soak in the bath. Then if you do want something, there's plenty in the fridge."

"That's a good idea. I'll have a bath and then see. God, Ross!"

"I know, my love. Go on. Upstairs."

But when Ross went upstairs himself half an hour later to find out if his beloved Mike wanted a meal from the freezer, he found Angells wrapped in a damp towel, fast asleep on the bed. He gently rolled him over and, covering him as best he could, sighed sadly and finished the day as he'd started it.

"I'm sorry. I'm so sorry," he whispered.

* * *

The CID room was packed the following morning. They'd all got the message, uniformed as well as CID. Fortune and Flaxby sat near each other, near the door of the chief inspector's office. Angells, in a smart navy suit not black leathers, sat next to his uniformed opposite number.

The super cut straight to the quick. He was in majestic form.

"Those of you with mates who aren't here, make sure they know what's going on, and be careful where you do it. Walls have ears, especially in pubs."

A mobile rang.

"Switch that bloody thing off and listen. I'll spell it out so that even the dumbest of you will understand what we might be up against."

As briefly as possible, he explained what had happened and what would happen, and prepared everyone for the investigation that might follow. It was, at the moment, at a purely informal, fact-finding stage, due to the DSI referral, but if there were a full IPCC case to answer, everyone would finish up feeling tense and under pressure, not just those left reeling at the investigation's centre.

"So that's the state of play at the moment. Informal—relatively. No accusations. Just establishing the facts. Any questions?" There were none, so Flaxby turned to Angells and said, "Right, Inspector, go and powder your nose."

This was the nearest the super had ever come to publicly alluding to the inspector's sexuality. Eyes looked at eyes, and Angells himself, who rarely queried a Flaxby directive, looked at the super and said, "If you're goin' to talk about me, I'd rather stay and hear it."

"I'd rather you didn't. Out. Order."

The inspector slowly stood up and left, quietly closing the door. More than one person in the room envied his easy elegance and his self-control. Nobody envied his situation.

"That lot upstairs, they're congratulating themselves that the officer who's been most involved in dealing with the dead lad is the least likely of all of us to be nasty to him. They'll be patting themselves on the back with rainbow coloured gloves telling the press—cos the press will love this—that we're a really far-sighted Force and look how being gay doesn't stop that climb up the promotional ladder et cetera, et cetera. That's why we do the proper work and they just fart in their pants."

Despite the gravity of the situation, several of those present smiled. If farting in one's pants was the criterion for being one of the 'lot upstairs', then one or two of the senior officers in the room were on the wrong floor.

"The papers, the media, they're going to have a field day digging up stuff on the inspector. Everything from what he has for breakfast to how many times a day he shits. So, you don't discuss him in the canteen. Or the lavs. Or the locker room. Or the car park. You don't even talk about him in your sleep. Angells is absolutely no-go. Understand?"

He glared at every person seated and standing

in the room, one person at a time. There was absolute quiet.

"I'll take that as understood completely then. Be kind to Sunny here, and be kind to Sally. They've found themselves caught up in this. They didn't choose to be. And if you can't be kind to that one out there"—he gestured to the door—"at least be neutral and watch what you say to him."

And with that, Flaxby, having told Fortune he wanted a word, marched out of the CID room and into his office.

"Back to work, I guess," said Fortune to the assembled crowd, and followed him.

"I obviously can't keep him on the Coverham case, Ron," said Flaxby. "Not when he's at the centre of an inquiry."

Fortune said, "Of course not."

"You'll have to take it over."

"Solely because there's no one else who's senior enough," remained unspoken, and both men knew that seniority, not capability or desirability, lay uppermost in the super's mind. Flaxby had a second reason for taking Angells off the case too, but he was the only one aware of it. He was still wondering about those fingers down the throat.

Mike's lying, he thought. *And he's lying to me, and I don't like that one bit. It affects us all. I wish to God I knew what was in the bugger's head.*

* * *

At that precise moment, various people were filing past Angells in the corridor where he'd been waiting, leaning against the wall. He didn't register their passing. What *was* in his head was the thought that this case was far from over. It would just contain a different brief.

In one sense, Angells had quite medieval ideas on crime and punishment. He believed in pain. It wasn't the pain of the rack though, nor of hot metal drawn across bare flesh. Rather, he believed in pain of the mind. A lifetime of remorse fuelled by self-knowledge. Now, that was a sentence worth passing. It didn't mean that those who perpetrated crimes could never be happy. There could be plenty of happiness, but at some point every day for the rest of their lives, they'd be brought to their knees by self-disgust. They would plead for forgiveness—from whom, Angells wasn't sure— but there'd be no release till death. However, in real life, sentencing lay with the courts.

So why was David Falconer, the bastard who'd nearly wrecked Mike and Ross's lives, walking around freely when his son lay in pieces in the morgue? God, because of him Mike had come close to walking out and leaving Tunhead, so close.

And he began to join the dots and make connections, and he saw that there might be a way to get Falconer into court and get him into jail, and get inside his head and cause him the pain he deserved. So he stood in the corridor, lost in these thoughts, until one of the DCs said "Sir?" for the second and louder time, and Angells realised he was wanted on the phone.

* * *

A long, trying day, and Angells should have been glad to drive home, but one thing weighed on him so heavily and crushingly that he almost wished he could stay in Warbridge. How was he going to tell his three men that he'd been unfaithful? To someone who was critical of somebody in a four-way relationship, this might have seemed the height of fatuity. Why not add a fifth body to the mix? But the four men were loyal, and faithful, to each other. A quartet was fine, a quintet undesirable, and this was even worse. It had all the dirty smell of a fast one behind the bike sheds.

Confessions, thought Angells. *How hard it is to make one, now the boot is on the other foot.*

Should he tell them at all? It had simply been the situation—two men overwhelmed by the emotions generated. It hadn't been a question of temptation or lust or a hunger for a young, firm, supple body. But try as he might to convince himself that, in a sense, he hadn't been unfaithful—no intention, no *mens rea*—he could still see the trail of clothes strewn on the floor, smell the lube on his fingers, hear the young man's moans as he'd checked he was ready... What was all that if it wasn't being unfaithful? *No wonder unfaithfulness is included in the grounds for dissolvin' a civil partnership,* Angells thought bitterly. *They know we can't be fuckin' trusted.*

So he reached home still wondering. Could he handle living with yet another lie?

He couldn't lie to Ross.

Ross sensed Angells looking at him. "Is there something you need to tell me?" he asked.

Angells nodded. Ross raised his eyebrows inquisitively and waited.

"I love you," said Angells.

"I know you do. Is that all you were going to say?"

"No."

You don't have to tell him.

But I do.

"I fucked Thijs Falconer. I'm so sorry."

"Oh."

Ross spent a minute gazing out of the window and tapping his fingers on the arm of the chair.

"I told you to be careful," he said gently.

Angells looked stunned. "Is that what you meant? You thought I might?"

"More than 'might', Mike. What about Phil and Raith?"

"I haven't told them yet. I will do, but I wanted to tell you first."

Ross nodded.

"You're an idiot, Mike, do you know that? At least I had the good sense to fuck *my* dead boy *before* I met you. Does this make us quits? Perhaps it does."

* * *

Phil

Practicalities initially threw Mike and myself together. If it was winter and he was on a late shift or he had a really early start, it sometimes made no sense to try to travel home. The main road, the 689, is drivable provided the gritters have been out, but once one turns off at Tunhope... well, that little road up the side of the beck is awkward at the best of times. It becomes steep, it's winding. Hit a patch of black ice and God knows how one would end up— not in one piece, that's for certain.

So, one evening, when Mike was at the hospital officially and outside it resembled the Arctic more than England, even more than north-east England, I said he could overnight at my house if he wished to. He'd probably have declined, but it transpired that

Ross was in Birmingham or somewhere, finalising details for a show, so there was no one to go home to anyway.

It became the norm. Bad weather, my house. At first he used a spare bedroom. Then, on one occasion, he just seemed very low. A hard day, a case that was preying on his mind. He drank more than he meant to and his defences were down. Obviously we didn't fuck—as I say, he was tired and tipsy—but he let himself lie in my bed in my arms and we kissed and cooed until he fell asleep. I thought that, maybe, next morning, he'd feel awkward and embarrassed and neither he nor I would know what to say.

When I woke he was still sleeping, so I tiptoed down the stairs to make a cup of coffee. The sounds of crockery clanging and water rushing through the pipes must have disturbed him, for a couple of minutes later he came downstairs too, already fully dressed. He opened the curtains, and it resembled a Christmas card scene outside—clean, thick snow covering everything.

He said, "Do you know what I'd like to do? Build a snowman."

And that's what we did. Laughing and chucking snowballs at each other, falling about in the snow and building a snowman. Two grown men! Totally daft and totally wonderful. I've a selfie of us standing either side of the snowman, our arms round its shoulders.

I don't know what he told Ross but, whatever it was, Ross didn't hold it against him and he didn't hold it against me either. I met Ross for the first time a few weeks later, and the only reference he made to the fact that his partner had admitted that he was intending to occasionally sleep with someone else was to ask me to handle Mike with care because he was very special. I promised I would, and I've kept my promise. He is special. A lovely man. He has a quality that I've never known in any other person. Raith's not far wrong when he calls him 'Angel Baby'.

Chapter 11

Although a full IPCC investigation had not yet been deemed necessary, a heaviness blanketed the CID room on the morning that the IPCC representative was due to arrive. At any other time of any other day, moans, groans and curses would have been the sounds to emanate from overworked officers at cluttered desks. That morning though, conversation was subdued and the atmosphere was tense. The inspector was popular. So too were DCs Sanghera and Topley. Was there a case to answer? Was there evidence of misconduct? Of unsatisfactory performance? An indication of criminality? Had any of the three behaved in a manner which would justify disciplinary proceedings? By the end of the day, everyone would be closer to finding out.

Sanghera was first to be interviewed. Introductions were made. The IPCC representative was a retired chief superintendent named Bellman who'd spent his working life in a Midlands division. Sanghera was assured (reassured, because Flaxby had already drummed the fact into him) that this was simply a preparatory fact-finding mission to see if there might be a case to answer, and he was asked to repeat, in detail, everything that had happened at Cinderella's and subsequently at the station when Thijs Falconer had his first interview.

Sunny was adamant that neither physical nor psychological pressure had been brought to bear on the young man. Everything was as it should have been.

"PACE-perfect," he said. "It wouldn't be anythin' else with Inspector Angells. He always plays by the book."

Flaxby smiled encouragingly. *Nice one, Sunny*, he thought.

"What did you think of the witness's state of mind?" Mr Bellman asked when Sanghera had finished making his report.

"I don't know," the young constable said thoughtfully, adding without any mockery, "I'm not a psychiatrist, but if I had to make a supposition, I'd say he was very anxious and nervous. Partly because he wasn't over bright, if you know what I mean. He was a bit bewildered by everythin'. And, his boyfriend had died, though we only realised that later."

"Did either you or the inspector try to put him at ease?"

"The inspector repeated that we were just tryin' to find out what had happened, that we weren't tryin' to accuse him of anythin'. Oh, and he got him a cup of tea and he had one too."

Despite the gravity of the situation, Flaxby couldn't help a smile. Of course, he didn't know that there had been other reasons for the need of some refreshment.

"Did that help?"

"A bit."

"Was he more nervous than any other witness might be?"

"Well, no one likes to be brought in for questionin', but I'd say he was more fidgety than most, yes."

"Why do you think that was?"

"I don't know, sir." Spoken thoughtfully again. No hint of impatience or insolence as none was intended.

"Do you think that his being a gay man had anything to do with his fear?"

"Bein' gay? You mean, he might have thought that there's a bit of history between the Force and the gays, and he might get beaten up in a cell?" Sundeep queried.

"That's the sort of possibility that occurred to me."

"Well, not *now*, sir, and anyway, sir," protested the constable, "the inspector's gay."

"But I presume that Inspector Angells didn't tell him so."

"Well, no, he didn't. So I suppose it might have worried him, then, but if so, he was worryin' unnecessarily," said Sanghera with loyalty to the Force, to Angells, and with certainty.

"What about your own attitude toward the gay community, Detective Constable?"

The gay community, thought Flaxby. *Stupid phrase. It makes people sound as though they're not part of normal society—separate, weird. Though what's a better term? The very medical sounding 'homosexuals'? Androphiles?* He'd heard that one was catching on.

"To LGBT in general, sir, why should I have an attitude? People are people. I admit I felt a bit awkward in Cinders, sir, but I think that's natural. I mean, we were undercover waitin' for the suspect to come in and someone asked me to dance, which was embarrassin'."

Flaxby concealed a second smile at the thought of Sanghera, the station's straightest man, setting the dance floor alight. He was desperate to know if the DC had taken up the offer of a tango but he'd have to hold his tongue on that one—for now, at any rate.

And the lad was doing well. He'd fended off the loaded attitude question with aplomb.

"The only gay man I know well is Inspector Angells and, I mean, I don't know him socially or anythin'. I mean in a work sense, and I've got the greatest respect for him, sir."

Another nice one, lad, thought Flaxby. *Got the makings of a chief constable with all that tact you're showing.*

"All right, DC Sanghera. Thank you. I think, Superintendent, I'd like to speak to DC Topley now."

"Right," said Flaxby. "Straight to the canteen. OK?"

"Yes, sir. Thank you," said Sanghera, before he left.

Well, thought Flaxby, *if they're all as straightforward as that, we're all OK. Have my doubts, though.* He cast a sideways glance at the ex-chief super to see if he could read anything from his features, but he was making notes and giving nothing useful away. Flaxby rang for Topley.

Sundeep Sanghera had been nervous of appearing before the Commission simply because, ipso facto, it was a Commission, a pre-Commission at any rate. True, he'd felt uneasy because of the way the interview with Falconer had ended, but as he pointed out, the thinking behind that was that the man could be recalled, the next day if need be.

Sally Topley was far less nervous of the Commission per se. She figured she could hold her own with any man or woman who wished to grill her. Her anxiety was due to the knowledge that being truthful could cause problems for the inspector.

"It wasn't a typical statement-type interview, no," she admitted, reluctantly. "Usually, I ask questions and he listens. Then he goes over the same ground and I listen for discrepancies. Sometimes he goes first, but usually, I do. This time, I just listened. Also, when I say he asks questions, it's not Bang! Bang! Bang! It's wait, wait, wait. He either makes it so uncomfortable that people seem to answer just to fill the silence, or he looks at them very encouragingly and they talk anyhow. A sort of confessional. It's just something he's able to do. I can't really explain it. But with Falconer, he asked a lot of closed questions. 'Did you? Were you? Then you did such and such, did you?' He didn't give him the same opportunity to talk freely as usual, and he filled up the silences himself."

Topley looked at Flaxby, agonised. He could see she hated saying this, as it begged the question: why the difference? But, it was all perfectly clear on the interview tape. You only had to listen. They both knew she had no choice.

Flaxby wanted her out of the room with as little further questioning as possible. He invisibly breathed a sigh of relief when she was finally sent to the canteen to commiserate with her colleague. Given the rather damaging nature of her comments, it was felt that a break was needed before continuing the inquiry by interviewing the inspector himself.

The ex-chief super was familiar with Angells' service record, but he glanced through a copy to refresh his memory as he sipped a cup of station coffee.

"Interesting man, Superintendent," he ventured. "A dedicated officer."

"And what makes you say that?"

"Several Crown Court Commendations—for bravery and for the way he's put together his cases—Chief Constable's Commendations, an RHSA for bravery…"

"Yes, that would be when he jumped into a swollen river to rescue a young lad who was drowning in it. Off-duty that was, and the other bravery one's from when he put his body in front of a shotgun held by a bugger who'd just shot a security guard at a warehouse near here."

"…and several mentions regarding initiative…"

"Yes, he's not short on initiative."

"…and his police exams. He must have some of the highest scores ever. Not uni though."

"No. Chose not to go and worked his way up to inspector. It's obvious what he's made of. He's a bright man and a good detective. He'll go further as long as…" Flaxby let his sentence remain unfinished, as both he and the ex-chief super knew exactly what he meant. Instead, he said, "I've sometimes thought that if Burke and Hare had managed to rob Angells' grave and give his brain to Doctor Knox to dissect and analyse, we'd have solved half the world's problems by now. Trouble is, we'd have caused another half."

Mr Bellman allowed the super's enigmatic comment to pass by without a comment of his own.

"OK, Superintendent Flaxby, can you call Inspector Angells, please?"

* * *

"Inspector," said Mr Bellman, when the introductions had been made, "I'd like to go straight to an observation of DC Topley's regarding the way you conducted the interview with the witness on the morning of the twenty-fourth."

Angells nodded and waited for a question.

"The constable tells me that you and she often conduct interviews together."

Angells confirmed this with another nod and a politely spoken, "Yes, sir."

"Apparently, she often takes the first part of a session. You take over and recap and ask further questions in order to clarify issues or elicit more information?"

"That's right, sir. Yes."

"That's not what happened this particular time?" It was phrased as a question.

"No, sir," Angells said by way of a reply.

"Inspector, if you are only going to tell me yes and no, we're not going to get very far very quickly. Please tell me why you adopted a different method of conducting the interview from the one that you and DC Topley usually employ."

Angells had known this question would arise. He knew he was going to have to lie. He knew all about those cognitive behaviour tricks, staring off into the top left corner of the room as though recalling and replaying a scene, and he felt he could possibly con his visitor, but what about Flaxby? He wondered if the super would see that he was lying. He hated himself for what he was about to do. He hoped his guilty feelings wouldn't give him away.

"I couldn't go in harder," said Angells after some seconds' pause. "He was scared, not just in the way suspects are always a bit scared. He'd just lost his lover. Wasn't just a fling. They'd been together for three years. He was sufferin'. Bereaved. After three years of secrecy. All bottled up inside him. I felt I had to be gentle."

Flaxby looked at him. Angells? Interview room? Gentle?

"Couldn't DC Topley have been equally gentle?"

"I understood where he was comin' from in a way that… I don't know what you know about me."

"I know enough to know that you might be admitting the possibility that you allowed personal feelings to interfere with your professional activities. Would that be an accurate description?"

"Yes, sir," Angells said quietly.

"And that DC Topley realised. Did you know that?"

"Yes, sir. I guessed," he admitted dejectedly.

"Which placed her in a compromising situation."

"I know, sir," he said with genuine misery. He'd hated himself for involving his junior colleague in his deception.

"Were you satisfied that Thijs Falconer was not responsible for John Coverham's death?"

Without hesitation, Angells repeated his, "Yes, sir."

"Did you ask him sufficiently penetrating questions to establish his innocence beyond all doubt?"

Now there was a hesitation.

"In all honesty, maybe not, sir."

Flaxby looked at him again. Angells? Interview room? Uncertain?

"So, we seem to be back to your feelings."

"Sir, look. He's scared. He's not fully with it anyway. He's not simple but he's not fully aware. He's lost the man he loves. It all had to be kept secret—their affair—cos there's so many bloody bigots around. Even now. They'd kept it secret for three years. We're supposed to take vulnerability into account when we interview a suspect, aren't we? Well, he was vulnerable. What would you want me to do? Squeeze him like he was some sort of serial killer?"

Oh Jesus, Angells, shut up, thought Flaxby. *You're not helping yourself.*

"Find out the truth, of course. Not act in a possibly unprofessional manner. There's no answer to that, Inspector. Your empathy and his vulnerability are no excuse for lack of reasonable pressure."

"No? Look, sir. You want to know if we acted heavy-handed or not. Did what we did contribute to Thijs Falconer's suicide? Establishin' the facts that led to the DSI—that's the main point of this interview, isn't it? Not an investigation into my feelin's. Not an investigation into Falconer's guilt or innocence."

Mike, stop telling him what his job is, willed Flaxby. *Even though you're right.*

"Well we weren't heavy-handed," said Angells angrily. "Sanghera, Topley, there's no way they'd come on too heavy. And I certainly didn't. You reckon my feelin's got in the way and that therefore I acted unprofessionally." *Jesus*, he thought, *you don't know how unprofessionally*. "And if that's what you think then I'll take whatever rap you and the chief constable and the Commission think I ought to take for that. But, please, leave those two out of it. I was the superior officer. It was all down to me. Nuthin' to do with them."

Flaxby was looking at the ceiling. He could see a neat way out of this.

"Wait outside please, Inspector," said Mr Bellman firmly.

"Sir."

Angells nodded and, apparently mastering his anger, quietly left the room without even glancing at the two men seated at the table.

"Superintendent Flaxby, this is very awkward," said the ex-chief super.

No doubt about that, thought Flaxby. *And a good job it is awkward, too.*

"Inspector Angells is correct. From the narrow point of view of the IPCC remit, all three of your officers clearly acted in accordance with PACE procedures. Indeed, they abided by the directive to take into account an interviewee's state of mind. I can therefore recommend that there is no case to answer. However, regarding Angells' lack of professionalism, which he admits, if we leave here and your soft-hearted gay inspector gets publicly hauled over the coals or demoted for acting unprofessionally because he empathised with a vulnerable gay suspect then we put police/LGBT relations back years, don't we?"

"If you hadn't said that, I would have," said Flaxby, "Won't just be bridges collapsing either. There are still some nasty buggers up there who don't like the idea of having a Force full of gay men. Slight exaggeration, but you know what I mean. The way Angells dealt with this—it was certainly wrong, but it's just the sort of grist to the mill those bigots are looking for. My suggestion would be to let us deal with Angells quietly and internally." *He certainly needs something thrust up his bloody ass*, he thought. "Right now, I'm not sure how, but I'll make certain he realises how lucky he is to stay in his post."

* * *

Two hours later, following a meeting between Bellman, Flaxby and the CC, the result of which was an agreement to play down 'The Angells Affair', Angells was called into Flaxby's office again.

The super pointed to a chair, and Angells sat down.

"Well, got anything useful to say?" Flaxby asked,

boring a hole through the inspector's forehead.

"Nuthin'. Sir. I'm sorry," said Angells contritely. "I shouldn't've let fly like that."

"Seems to me you shouldn't have done a lot of things, and you should have done a lot of others."

Angells nodded.

"Is this goin' to a full-on investigation? Am I suspended?" he asked quietly.

"No, it isn't, and no, you're not suspended. Yet," Flaxby added threateningly. "I've told you: being gay's no problem as long as it doesn't come between you and your job. And it has. You didn't do your job properly. You should have pressed more. You let a suspect walk free because you felt sorry for him. I mean, for God's sake, Mike! This isn't the bloody Sally Army. We can't be feeling sorry for people."

"I couldn't break his story, sir. He was out of the frame," said Angells stolidly.

"You couldn't or you wouldn't? What did you really think? Did Falconer do it?"

Angells' mind was racing. As long as they thought that there were only feelings and strong emotion at the bottom of this and not something far more dangerous, then he could take whatever they dealt him. He wasn't being suspended. He wasn't being demoted. He just had to stay calm and handle the bollocking he knew could come, but tension had built up too much. Probably just as well, because it got him out of answering Flaxby's question.

"It doesn't matter what I thought, does it?" he said defiantly. "I'm gay, remember. It affects my judgement."

"And I'll throw insubordination at you as well if you want. Don't be an idiot as well as everything else. This is *me* you're talking to, Mike. And thank God you *are* gay, because the only thing keeping this within the department is that we don't want the Rainbow Brigade to hold you up as some sort of bloody martyr to the cause. So consider yourself lucky. Bloody lucky. Oh, shove off, Inspector, and keep out of my way till I know what to do with you. Go on. Get!"

"Sir."

How bloody stupid, thought Angells as he returned to his little office. Twenty years before, he'd have lost his job because he was gay. Now he was told he was keeping it for the same reason. Perhaps ten years into the future, all police would *have* to be gay, or bi, or transgender or something. An entry requirement. And, yes, he realised he was lucky. If he *had* been suspended, it would have made it impossible to carry out the rest of his plan to put David Falconer behind bars. As it was, he could keep well out of the super's way—he'd been told to—and get on with executing it. But relief soon changed to despondency. He was glad that things had turned out the way they had but, in equal measure, dismayed that he *was* glad. Lying to everyone. Going along with the idea of empathy and feelings. There was some truth in that, he knew, but it wasn't feelings that had dictated his actions and approach, was it? Not feelings for Thijs Falconer, anyway.

At home, Angells ate his evening meal silently and absently. Then he sat staring at the TV screen for an hour, clearly clueless about the content of the transmission, and it was no surprise to Ross when he said, "I'm turning in early, Ross," and went upstairs to bed. He was still awake when Ross retired an hour or so later, and long after Ross's breathing showed that he was fast asleep, Angells still lay there, eyes open, gazing miserably at the ceiling and at what he saw inside himself.

* * *

Phil

Blay Fenn Prison. Right then; here we are—a somewhat embroidered tale. It's been told with variations several times in the last fifteen years or so, and I'm not certain what parts of it are facts and which are the products of Raith's fertile imagination! I'm assured that this is the truth in essence! So here we go:

He stood there with that sullen "Sod you. Seen it all before and I don't care Jack Shite" look on his face. Up before the magistrates for the umpteenth time. This particular magistrate, looking through the catalogue of offences and their clearly ineffectual punishments, was pleased to see that the obvious waste of public time and space and money called Raith Balan (an Anglicised version of Balaño) had added GBH to the lengthy list. She passed the case to the County Court, where the judge decided that the provocation (that Raith's mum had had it off with all eleven players of Raith Rovers first team, and hence his name) did not warrant the response (a series of kicks and thumps so fierce that, had there been a net, the provocateur, minus teeth, would have sailed right through it and landed in the stands.) So Raith found himself sent down for two years and en route to Blay Fenn along with three other convicted souls. The one who'd been there before was very quiet during the journey.

Possessions confiscated, various orders given, papers shoved in front of his nose that he signed without reading, and Raith was taken to his new home. The heavy door was closed behind him. The two men already in the cell looked him up and down. One slowly walked round him, then stood a yard or so in front of his face and punched it.

"You fucker!" said Raith, recovering his balance and rubbing his cheek.

"I mean to be," said the puncher.

"Shit!" said Raith, who'd been inside enough juvenile detention centres and youth wings to know that when a cellmate with a tiger tattooed across his bare scalp sets out his intentions, you didn't call for a prison guard's help.

And the other man merely offered a sardonic smile and said, "Well when you do, it'll probably hurt. I'm Joe, by the way."

So that night, Raith found himself being buggered for the very first time but, before the week was out, he found he didn't need the sock his cellmates had stuffed in his mouth in case his objections were too vociferous. What's more, Tiger Head and Joe ensured that no one else stuck a penis up him. Or anything else for that matter.

Blay Fenn was full of surprises for Raith. Not only did he discover that he was if not gay then certainly bi, he discovered he had talent. The discovery began with a drawing.

"When you get out," he said to Tiger Head one afternoon, "you should have something like this tattooed on you. If you can find a bit of bare skin, anyway."

He passed over a piece of paper on which he'd drawn a detailed picture of a lioness bringing down some sort of deer.

"'S fucking good, that," said Tiger Head admiringly. "Do us another."

"What of?" asked Raith.

"Draw him!" commanded Tiger Head. "Come on, Joe. Pose for Picasso here."

"How come you didn't say you could do this stuff?" asked Joe when he looked at what was an accurate likeness of himself.

"Never thought much about it," Raith answered. "You think it's good then?"

And the upshot of that was that Joe, who was actually quite fond of the big, exotic-looking creature whom they sodomised most nights, got Raith into the art therapy classes available to him as a long-stretch inmate, classes that were theoretically denied to Raith on his shorter sentence. At that point, at the age of twenty-one, Raith Balan's world turned round.

The art tutor's name was Miss Brown, though the inmates called her Miss B.

"Miss B says I'm a tetramat or something," Raith told his cellmates some weeks later.

"Some kind of laundry?"

"No! She wrote it down. Look."

He passed over a piece of paper on which the art tutor had written the word "tetrachromat."

"Tetrachromat, you stupid bugger. Can't you read? What's it mean anyway?"

"She says it means that I can see more colours than most people. Like you see pale green, I see pale greens. Or something."

"What good's that going to do you when you get your arse out of here?" asked Tiger Head.

"Don't know. She says I should go to art college."

"You! Get yourself a fucking gun, not a fucking paint brush. Don't be an asshole."

"Very funny."

That night, there were problems.

"What the fuck's the matter with you tonight?" Tiger Head demanded.

"I don't want to. No—fuck off yourself," Raith shouted, pushing his cellmate away.

He was dragged off the bed and punched hard in the stomach.

"Leave him be, Ti," said Joe. "Leave him be. Come on."

Ti let himself be led away, though not without having issued a threat.

"You've got six months to go in here yet. Don't forget it."

Raith closed his eyes to the finger that was in his face. "I'm not forgetting it," he said.

A few days later, as he watched a lump of clay take shape in Raith's hands, Joe asked, "Are you going to go to this college then?" Raith couldn't just draw and paint. He could make the clay do exactly what he wanted it to.

Raith shrugged. "I'd like to, but…" Another shrug.

"You're fucking stupid if you don't," Joe continued. "It'd keep you out of here. Give you a bit of a future. You're young enough to have one. Unless you want to spend your life getting slack-arsed in a shithole like this."

Raith liked Joe. He was surprised and he was touched by his cellmate's concern, but there was no way he was going to even begin to explain his reluctance to take his new-found talent any further. Some things you kept to yourself, and the facts that he could hardly read and couldn't spell were two of them. They were the basis of his hatred of school, of his boredom there, of his annoyance, of everything that was wrong with his life. They were the reasons he'd got in with the crowd he'd mixed with. They were, in a sense, what had brought him to Blay Fenn. In sheer frustration at what he felt was to be his unfair lot in life, he picked up the piece he'd been working on and hurled it across the room. A guard—there were always two—came racing over.

"That's enough of that, you fucker! Back home! Come on!"

"It's all right," said Miss B, quickly interposing herself between the guard and Raith, whose fists, she could see, were clenched tight. "Let's put it down to artistic temperament. No report needed."

She took Raith firmly by the arm before the guard could object, and sat him down at a table as far away from anyone else as the confines of the room would permit.

"What was that about?" she asked calmly.

"You and the fucking college you keep on at me about," he found himself saying. "I want to, but I can't. I can't read."

He waited for some outpouring of surprise, scorn, horror. All he got was a very matter-of-factly spoken, "That's not a problem," and she proceeded to explain why it wasn't.

"So you see," she said, "a disproportionate number of people who are artistic and creative have what are commonly called dyslexic tendencies, and now that this is recognised, measures are in place to ensure that dyslexic students are accommodated."

"What sort of measures?" he asked, interested albeit sullen.

"Lectures can be taped so you don't have to write them up. Your own essays can be scribed. You can have someone to support you to help you research material in the library. Just to help you organise yourself if necessary. Get to where you should be at the right time. And there'd be several people getting that sort of support, so you wouldn't feel singled out in any way."

She could see he was considering this. *Come on, Raith,* she willed. *Make a stand. Take control.*

"Would they have me? With my record? And I don't have any exams or anything."

"They'd interview you and they'd look at a

portfolio of your work and they'd talk to us here, and, yes, I'm sure they'd have you. They'd be mad not to. You're a real talent. You're observant, and you have a wonderful ability to transfer what you observe onto canvas and to clay. Really, you're good."

Come on, Raith. Say yes.

"Look, it's not a life sentence. If you don't like it, you can quit, but if you get out of here with nothing else, you could find yourself back in and you won't get a second chance."

So, four years later, Raith Balan, bisexual ex-con, graduated from the University of Newcastle with a first in Fine Art and walked straight into a job assisting a well-known sculptor to prepare and execute his many commissions. True, it had taken him four years to complete a three-year course, as halfway through the final year he'd had a total meltdown, destroyed most of his 3D project work and had to repeat the year again, but with a great deal of counselling and sensitive support, he got himself together and began to go up in the world.

At least, that's how Raith told me the current version!

Chapter 12

Later, Mike would think that the Fates had listened in on the following conversation and, in thinking *that's an intriguing idea*, made real the idea and brought it to pass.

"Mike, the Coverham case is still open, isn't it?" Ross asked. "Obviously so, in view of the fact that we are two of the only three people alive who know that it should be closed. You say your dear DCI Fortune has been put on the case. What would you do if he started to chase someone? Someone innocent?"

"He might be a shiter but I don't think he'd set some poor sod up just to keep his case-solved stats high. Anyway, I think the super would be wise to that."

"I'm sure he would," said Ross reassuringly. "I meant, rather, what if Fortune pursued somebody in error and the evidence seemed to fit? What would you do?"

"Find some way to change his mind. I'd have to, wouldn't I?"

"You wouldn't just stand by?"

"No! What sort of cop do you think I am?"

Shit, he suddenly thought. *What sort of cop do I think I am? Now: as dishonest as any I've known.*

"I just wondered if you'd thought this through as far as that."

"Yes. I have," Angells said flatly. "I wouldn't let someone get fingered for Thijs Falconer's crime, if that's what you're thinkin'. Evidence 'ud have to be just circumstantial, wouldn't it? I mean, it couldn't be anythin' else, seein' we know who's responsible. I'd have to make sure Ron Fortune 'ud see it'd get thrown out of court."

"But if you leave and the case is still unsolved?"

"*When* I leave. I can't stay. We both know that. Eventually the trail'll go cold and there'll be sumthin' else to get hot under the collar about. Even a high-profile one like this."

So Angells went to work, shortly after the IPCC referral interview, and found himself at loggerheads with DCI Fortune. Just as Ross had thought might happen, Fortune was chasing an innocent man.

As Ross had, unnecessarily, pointed out, John Coverham's death was still part of an ongoing, unsolved investigation, and because of its high profile, it was one that was creating a great deal of extra pressure on already loaded shoulders. Fortune, plagued by calls from the chief constable and determined to show her that he was a better detective than Angela, had read, re-read and read again the various witness statements and department reports, but nothing he saw there seemed to offer any new clue. Then PC Rogers, one of the uniformed staff who'd been drafted in to help go through the information gleaned from street cameras, knocked on his office door and offered what might be a lead. Niall Tomlinson, the man he and PC Jacobs had brought back to the station some weeks previously because he'd been shouting obscenities outside Manny's Bar, was clearly visible on three of the street cams near Manny's late in the morning of the day John

Coverham had died. Fortune had Tomlinson brought in for questioning, if only to eliminate him from enquiries.

He didn't really expect anything to come from the interview, so when a junior colleague tapped on the door and asked for a word outside, he was pleasantly surprised—Niall Tomlinson's prints were on the wall above the urinal in Manny's toilets and on the outside of the back door. He'd gone from being merely in the vicinity of the building; he could be placed inside it. A ray of light at last. Fortune could see a case building up. If Tomlinson had entered through the open back door knowing he could have a piss, if, being drunk or even sober, he had insulted Coverham, who was already operating at danger level because of his arguments with Falconer, or if his presence had been queried, if there had been a scuffle, if...

"That's too many ifs, Ron," Angells had argued when Fortune had called him in to inform him of these new developments. "You'll never get that past the CPS. They'll want this wino's DNA on Coverham's body, not just fingerprints on the wall and a load of ifs. It's all too circumstantial."

Oh God, it might not be, he was thinking.

"It is at the moment," Fortune responded, "but it's more than you turned up, and I'm running with it."

"It's nuthin' to go on!" said Angells, raising his voice.

"It's a lot more than that," said Fortune, becoming loud in turn. "A known homophobe who's created trouble at Manny's Bar before is in the gents around the time a man dies. And it is around the right time. We can exclude eleven thirty to twelve forty-five because he's caught on camera then. So, where was he between twelve forty-five and one fifteen, when Coverham's body is found? For some of the time in Manny's Bar, too, by the look of things."

"But where was he before eleven thirty?" Angells persisted. "He could have been in the gents then."

"Read your own report, man! They only opened that back door at eleven fifteen when they had a delivery. Then they left it open because it was a scorching day. He's at Bolton Street at eleven thirty. Five minutes in the gents. He couldn't have walked from Manny's to Bolton Street in ten minutes. There's no direct bus, and he's not going to get a taxi, is he?"

"He might've," said Angells obstinately, but ninety per cent certain that Tomlinson wouldn't have done so. *Shit*, he thought. *Shit. Shit. Shit.* "It's just not watertight enough. There's a dozen other explanations!"

"OK. If there's a dozen, give me one," Fortune shouted, annoyed that he should be yelled at by Angela and fed up of a case that wasn't going anywhere.

Something else that would fit the DCI's so-called facts…

"Well," said Angells, thinking as clearly as he could given the shock of this turn of events, "he could've left his prints in Manny's lav on another day, and he could've been somewhere where there weren't any street cams."

"In Warbridge? There are bloody cameras everywhere! You can't move for the bloody things."

"No there aren't," insisted Angells, remembering the street map he'd constructed for the Coverham briefing, "and they don't all work anyway. The bus station ones were out the day Coverham died. We couldn't get footage. Remember? *You* read the bloody report."

"Well, pissing in Manny's on another day and the cams out of action would be a real coincidence, wouldn't it?"

"Coincidences happen, Ron!" said Angells, thinking, *and the biggest one's Ross and the bloody Dutch connection.* At which point, Flaxby came bursting in.

"Which one of you's lost his rattle, then? What the hell's going on?"

His inspector and chief inspector both glared at him.

"Right," he said. "Ron—you first."

"We've a man in the interview room who's a likely suspect for the Coverham case—"

"And it's all circumstantial!" interrupted Angells argumentatively.

"Shut up," said Flaxby.

Angells did so.

"And the inspector here seems to be on a mission to give everyone at the CPS a holiday. Everyone we try to finger for the Coverham death, he wants to let walk and says, 'It's circumstantial. There's another explanation.'"

"Well?" said Flaxby, turning to Angells. "I know your heart's gone soft. Has your brain turned to jelly too?"

"It's circumstantial, sir," Angells said desperately.

"Say that again and I'll circumstance you— or something very similar! OK, Ron, how circumstantial? Christ! Now I'm saying it."

Fortune explained the timing and Tomlinson's background and said, "Well, what do you think, Clive?"

Flaxby looked at Fortune and looked at Angells. He was reading their faces as best he could, and his reading was more than half correct. Fortune he could understand. He was under enormous pressure to close out this case—Flaxby almost felt sorry for him. Almost, for he knew that one-upmanship was also a factor in play.

But Angells was now an onlooker, feeling slighted and, being a man who liked to tie up cases tightly, being bloody awkward too. No… Angells wasn't a man who took umbrage. When necessary, he was willing to swallow humble pie. It was that something else again, the thing Flaxby hadn't quite been able to put his finger on. So Flaxby looked from one to the other and decided.

"It's more than circumstantial," he said, "but it won't stand up in court yet. What you need is a confession, Ron. Come on, let's talk to this fellow together and get one. But if we don't…"

Of course you bloody will, thought Angells. Faced with both Flaxby and Fortune, even with just Flaxby, a man would confess to anything from killing Abel to pulling the trigger on JFK.

"…then Mike gets his way. The wino walks."

The chief inspector, feeling he had scored a victory, gave Angells a smug glance and left to go to the interview room.

Angells had one more try.

"Sir," he began.

"Inspector," said Flaxby threateningly, "if you're not careful, I'll chuck you out of the window, and that won't be circumstantial. It'll be a bloody fact. If you don't like it," he paused and then said slowly and emphatically, "do something about it." As he went after Fortune, he added over his shoulder, "and be bloody quick."

Angells didn't need to be told twice.

He returned to his own office. Well, what happened in that interview room was outside his control. Other things were inside it. He'd do what he could and, as Flaxby had commanded, he'd do them quickly. He made a list of things he had to accomplish, altered their order somewhat, and began to work his way through them.

He needed to chat with Balraj Singh, one of the crime scene officers who'd been at Manny's Bar. He'd do better with a visit than an internal phone call. Perhaps something would strike him as significant.

"Where exactly were the fingerprints, Bal?" Angells asked when he'd made his way downstairs and along the relevant corridor. He had, of course, already re-read the report, but he felt dialogue would be more helpful than written words and photographs.

"There was one on the outside of the door that opens onto the alley."

"How high? Can you demonstrate?"

Balraj did so and said, "It's consistent with pushing the door further open than it was when it was wedged open—which it was, because it was a hot day. There was another on the wall above the urinal. Left hand. Sideways on. The kind of position you might use if you had drunk too much and needed to lean against the back wall for support, forehead resting on hand."

"You mean: drunk, to steady yourself. Feet behind the drainage gulley?"

"Exactly."

"Drunk. That's interestin'. And were they clear or overprinted?"

"The one on the wall was clear as day. Plenty of pressure if you were leaning on your hand. The one on the door, only a partial. Less clear and overprinted, to some extent, with prints from two of the bar staff. Maybe they'd rushed out the back to see if anyone was still there."

Angells thanked Balraj for his information, returned to his office and phoned Manny's Bar. Yes, Will was there, and—hang on—yes, it was fine to visit.

He was greeted like an old friend. How pleasant that someone, at least, wasn't yelling at him.

What Angells wanted to know was, firstly, how often the wall above the urinal was washed.

"You're not doubling as Environmental, are you?" the barman laughed. "I know that Council Tax has been capped and stuff, but surely we still have a separate police force. Wait a sec, I'll get Ted. He does the lavs. He can tell you himself. Best I don't hear the answer if it's 'last year.'"

"Before you do," said Angells. "This back door—is it often left open?"

"Often? Well if it's a hot day, we leave it open for a bit, partly to get rid of any whiffs from the toilets. I mean, you can't get into the rest of the premises without coming through here, so access is only the lav itself and a storeroom for cleaning gear. The deliveries come in there, and the bins are out there too. The door swings both ways for easy access."

"So if someone went to the bins or helped with unloadin', they might want to push the door open from the outside? If they hadn't wedged it open, that is."

"Yes. It tends to swing shut. Do you want to see?"

"Please," said Angells.

"Here's Ted. He can show you and tell you about the cleaning at the same time. Inspector Angells, Ted. He was here over the death of the footballer. Remember?"

Ted did remember, yes. A gay, leather-clad CID inspector was not someone who would easily be forgotten.

Ten minutes later, Angells thanked the two men and, pleased with the information he'd obtained, rode back to the station, where he checked out old weather reports. He knew it had been hot the day that Coverham had died. It turned out that the previous day had been a real scorcher. That back door would have been wedged open then, too.

Next, having spoken first to PC Rodgers, he went to the incident room and dug out the relevant surveillance data. He wanted to see how Tomlinson was walking. Was he steady on his feet? Was he already the worse for wear?

Most of the cams held video tapes. *Too jerky,* thought Angells. At four frames a second, he couldn't gain a clear enough picture. A couple of cams used discs, however. Angells ran the discs through twice. Tomlinson looked purposeful enough. He'd used the pedestrian crossing at the corner of Bolton and Sefton Street, and it seemed to Angells that he would certainly have been alert enough to stand at Manny's urinal without having to steady himself with his free hand. So, given that the wall above the urinal hadn't seen any cleaning fluids for a fair old time, perhaps Tomlinson had left his fingerprints there on a different day. It didn't have to be on the day of the death. Any hot day around then when, perhaps, he *had* been drunk and had slipped in to relieve himself. For example, the day before, as Angells had suggested to Fortune.

He looked at his watch. Flaxby and Fortune had been in the interview room over an hour. Even with Flaxby playing a double game and holding things up, for that was how Angells had interpreted his super's words and actions, he knew he didn't have much more time.

PC Rogers tapped him on the shoulder.

"Sorry, sir," he said. "The tapes and the discs for the previous day have been re-used. No one saw any need to keep 'em. It's a shame."

That didn't surprise Angells, though it was more than a shame. If he could have shown that Tomlinson had been near Manny's on the Wednesday as well as the Thursday, he wouldn't have had to do what he did next.

"And you're sure that there's no sign of Tomlinson near Manny's Bar after twelve forty-five?"

"Not on the cams, no. Don't know where he got to. No sign anywhere. Vanished. I checked, like you said."

"Thank you anyway," said Angells, "and thanks for your help."

"That all, sir?"

"Yes," said Angells, standing up. "Got to go out."

Angells knew he didn't have to provide irrefutable proof of Tomlinson's movements. All he had to do was act as a good defence lawyer would and demonstrate a different interpretation of the evidence. So, what if, instead of heading towards Manny's Bar at 12.45 as Fortune assumed and hoped, Tomlinson had gone instead towards the bus station and 'vanished' on a bus? The fact that he might not have done was irrelevant in a way. There'd be no CCTV record from the bus station. As he'd reminded the DCI, that had been a problem when they'd been trying to find footage of Thijs Falconer's movements. And the lack of sightings from the street cams? Angells knew exactly where the street cams were. There were several on the main thoroughfares. What if, though, in the middle of that hot June day when the sun was at its height, Tomlinson had made his way along the shaded, narrow streets behind the shops and office blocks?

The directive to come to work in regular clothing no longer being needed, Angells was back to using his bike. He worked out a possible route then raced down to the car park and rode off to check it out.

He'd only need to pass the two street cams on the main road near the bus station if he kept to the back streets. As he rode along them, he kept a lookout for CCTV monitors owned by the premises on the route. There seemed to be three. He aimed to show that a man could make the journey to the bus station from Tomlinson's last sighting at 12.45 without being caught on camera. He hadn't the time to worry about the niceties of the Highway Code—no entry, one way... he didn't care. He rode, to pedestrians' annoyance, along the narrow pavements where the monitors suggested he should do so. Then, leaving the back streets behind, and close to the bus station, he screeched to a track rider's 180 degree turn and raced back to his starting point to begin the journey again.

This time, at each of the three CCTV stations, he skidded to a halt, ran into the building the monitors were attached to and, with ID at the ready, demanded to see the last ten minutes on the surveillance discs or tapes. He didn't appear on any of them, and no one argued with him when he said he wanted to take them away with him.

He didn't feel the need to see or commandeer the information on the two Council-owned street cams. He'd looked as he'd ridden past, and he was certain that their field of view was sufficiently restricted to allow a man on foot on the opposite pavement to pass by without being noticed.

With the third disc stored safely in his jacket pocket, he took out his mobile and sent Flaxby a text: *2nd explanation feasible.* He knew he needed to say no more, and so, relieved but breathless, he returned to the station.

He entered the car park quietly and, having disabled the bike, stealthily went up the stairs and into his room. He didn't want to meet the DCI on route. He didn't know what reaction he would get. He felt exhausted, completely wrecked. The IPCC business. This race against the clock. Everything. At his desk, he lay his head on his hands and, for the first time ever, fell asleep on the job.

He stirred when he felt his shin kicked, and opened his eyes to see the super sitting opposite him.

"Why were you so sure the wino didn't do it?" Flaxby asked bluntly.

"I wanted Ron to be sure, that's all, before it all got all official and into the hands of a sharp lawyer."

"Oh yes? Nothing else?"

Angells felt Flaxby's stare probing for answers. As long as it didn't find any.

"Such as, sir?"

Flaxby said nothing, but just continued to try to dissect him. Angells returned the stare, if not entirely steadily, then at least steadily enough to make Flaxby stand up and leave.

But at the door, he turned back and said, "You haven't asked if Tomlinson confessed," and left before Angells realised that, significantly, he hadn't.

* * *

He was glad to get home. Raith was spending the night at Phil's and it was just the two of them for the chicken pie and chips Ross had taken out of the freezer earlier. Later that evening, tired but pleasantly sated by the food and a bottle or two of pale ale, Mike told Ross some of the things that had happened in the day.

"I'll be honest, luv," he said. "At first this little voice said, 'Wait! The best solution for you and Ross is to let this wino take the rap.' I hit the desk with my fist clenched so bloody hard I yelled out, and then I had to stretch each finger to ensure I hadn't broken any. I've sunk low, but not that low. Not so's I'd let someone else take the rap. That's lousy, isn't it? That I'd even think it?"

"Not meritorious, I agree, but understandable, entirely understandable," said Ross. "The point is, you didn't let it happen. What would you have done if you hadn't been able to rectify the situation so promptly? Do you know?"

"If I hadn't been able to sort it? At the time, do you know, it didn't even cross my mind to think that far ahead. I just knew I had to act. Quick. Sittin' here now, I know what I'd've done, yes. Even with a confession, a smart lawyer can get a man off if holes can be torn in the statement's reliability. You know that happens."

Ross nodded.

"But someone like this Tomlinson wouldn't be able to afford such a luxury. I'd've paid for a smart lawyer myself. I couldn't't've told the truth, could I? Jeez, what an awful admission. What a mess. I feel like everythin's happenin' around me, and I'm racin' round tryin' to sort it all out: the Falconers, the train, the Complaints Commission, this Tomlinson bloke—all on top of all the other cases. It's like I'm tryin' to stuff loads of things into a box but the lid keeps poppin' open, and all the time, knowin'. Knowin'! I hate that."

He opened another bottle and stared at the sailing barge depicted on its label.

"I wish I could fuckin' sail away into oblivion on a boat like this," he said. "Not goin' to happen, is it?"

"As pleasant a way to go as any, I imagine, but not very practicable," said Ross.

There was a silence while both men tried to think of as little as possible. Ross broke it.

"As long as the case remains open"—he took a swig from Angells' bottle—"what will happen, Mike?" he asked. "How will it end?"

"If I don't get caught?"

"If you don't get caught."

Angells continued to stare at the bottle, not because he felt its pale golden contents would act as some sort of liquid crystal ball, but simply for somewhere to rest his tired eyes.

"Like I said the other day, eventually the trail'll go cold. At least no one'll need to go chasin' their own arses ragged lookin' for someone to collar. Coverham'll just be a stat on a list."

The effect on the trail wasn't what Ross had been wondering about, but he let what he had meant be ignored.

Angells downed a good ten minutes' drinking time in one long draught. "Anyway," he continued, "the sooner we can finger David bloody Falconer, the better. Flaxby knows things aren't what they seem, but also, I just hate showin' my face. I wish I was a table or a chair. Inanimate, without feelin's. I just feel so fuckin' awful. I don't want to not be there. That is, I want to be a cop. I love it, but I want to leave too. Oh, man, what a mess."

"I'm sorry, Mike. I know I keep saying it, but I really am."

Angells gave Ross a hug with his free arm. The other held his nearly empty bottle.

That's it, he thought. *If I could just fade into the*

wall, or the floor, or the ceilin', just be a thing and not have to have feelin's… but then he was aware of Ross, still tucked inside his arm, and the slight scent of Ross's shampoo, mixed with the scent of shower gel and the fabric softener Ross insisted they rinse their laundry with.

He buried his chin in Ross's thatch of hair, which tickled because it was curly, and he thought of walks along the beck and up the moors and of Ross's arm around *him* when he woke in the middle of the night, and if Ross hadn't stayed alert right then, the bottle would have dropped to the floor and spilt what beer it still contained, for—for the second time that day—Angells had fallen asleep where he sat.

Ross gently extricated himself and, equally gently, laid Angells down and raised his legs onto the sofa. Then he went upstairs to fetch a travel rug and tucked it round him. He placed a chair beside the sofa in case Angells rolled over and onto the floor in his sleep and, then, having kissed him on the forehead, went up the stairs again, to bed.

Several hours later, he felt Angells climb in beside him and, wrapped in each other's arms and legs, they slept like tired babes till they were woken by the sunlight in the morning.

* * *

Raith

Phil says that I fell victim to my own success. I suppose he's right.

Peri sometimes sat for the sculptor I worked for

when I left uni. It didn't take long before we were together, and I knew that I could do things with Peri, in paint and in clay, that were way better than what Ralph (my patron? my mentor?) was putting out.

There were the colours in his skin for a start. He was from Marseille and most people would say his skin was olive, but I saw dozens of greens and browns and other colours in it. And I saw silvers and shades of blue and purple in his black hair.

His body. He was in his early twenties, a year or so younger than me. He was slim and sleek. Just gorgeous to feel the clay under my hands copying the shapes of his arms and legs.

But he was a bastard. He was a right jealous sod, and if he thought I was looking at another man with sex on the brain, there'd be all hell to pay. God, we had some awful fights. When he realised he might be losing me to Angel Baby, he threatened to smash my hands in with a hammer. I'd had enough by then, and I felt more… powerful, I suppose. I told him to get out.

Angel Baby. So different from Peri, but the years pass and your tastes change. I liked him as soon as Ross introduced me to him.

"Ross has showed me some of your work," he'd said, making 'showed' sound like 'shored' and with a twinkle in his eyes that made me want to grab my paints there and then and get the movement and the colours onto canvas. And get him on to a bed—I thought he was bloody sexy. I didn't do either, though. Well, not straight away. I was still with Peri. In fact, I never did paint his eyes. The more I thought about it, the more I thought that perhaps I couldn't. I like a challenge, but I know when I'm beaten.

I liked the way he moved. I don't mean dancing! He's a bloody lousy dancer. I mean that he moved with assurance, with confidence. He had a job he liked and he was good at it. He had self-esteem and it spilled over into the way he carried himself, into everything about him, somehow. Not conceit. He's in no way a conceited man. It was just self-respect. I found it very attractive. Then, Ross talked about starting BOTWAC up, and it seemed an ideal move for me, so I ended up seeing a lot more of Angel Baby than I thought I would.

You couldn't get a more different agenda, could you? A CID detective who works within a really hierarchical structure surrounded by uniforms and laws and statutes and other Establishment paraphernalia, and a group of artists addicted to individualism and creativity (I heard Ross say that and I thought it sounded good) and who, literally, do their own thing. I suppose it helped that it wasn't a mass invasion. We trickled in. It must have been an upheaval even so, but he never complained, nor gave any of us the idea we were unwelcome additions to his little bit of paradise or whatever he thought it was. He took it all in his stride, in that quietly watchful way of his. You end up saying things to Angel Baby that you don't realise you're going to say, maybe don't even realise you're thinking, because he has this quiet calm about him. He draws things out of you. Thinking back to the old days, I wouldn't have liked to be on the other end of an interview with him. I'd have even grassed on folk I didn't know!

So when Peri went, I suppose I started spilling over into their property—his and Ross's—and, gradually, he started sitting for me, but no more than that. For a little time, anyway, no more than that.

Chapter 13

The evening after the tiring day that Mike had spent racing around to put Niall Tomlinson in the clear, he was sitting at home, sharing his thoughts about crime and punishment with Ross.

"I want to get the bastard, Ross," he said. "I want him banged up so much! Even if it's just for a short stretch."

"Well, why don't you make sure that the video that upset you, the one with the boy and his dad, finds its way onto Flaxby's desk?" asked Ross.

"No. I can't do that, can I? Thijs Falconer's name has to stay as dead as Thijs Falconer's body. I hate puttin' it crudely like that, but it's true. I can't risk it. It'd be openin' a can of worms. There was sumthin' on one of the videos, though. Sumthin' Coverham said."

In a lull between their activities, in a period of post-coital reflection, Thijs Falconer and the soccer player had discussed the content of the video the two of them had rigged up to film the father and son. It was obvious that they'd spoken of this before. Coverham was sympathetic, but neither surprised nor shocked.

"Well, at least we can thank him for all this," Coverham had said, airily gesturing at the room with the arm that wasn't embracing Thijs.

For all what? And why?

"I had a good look round Coverham's apartment when I got those videos," said Angells. "Fancy jewellery. Brochures for tailored holidays. Designer suits. Everythin' classy and top of the range. That video equipment itself must have cost thousands. I was envious! It's as good as anythin' I've seen downtown. And a smart car in the garage. Cost big money, and he shouldn't have got big money playin' at Ormerley. It's too small a team."

"So you think that, perhaps, there were some dodgy dealings that involved David Falconer?" asked Ross.

"Strange thing for Coverham to say otherwise, isn't it?"

Ross agreed. "I suppose the obvious thing is a betting scam," he said after a while. "One does hear of such things, and there are substantial sums involved."

Angells shook his head.

"That was one of the first lines of inquiry into Coverham's death," he said. "A scam turned nasty or sumthin'. We went through countless match reports, checked if he was carded at crucial stages in a match, spoke to the sports writers on the locals... If he was involved in some fixin' scam he certainly covered it up well. Feelin' was definitely that he was clean, though."

"Not a betting scam then. Not thrown matches," said Ross. "So how did he get his money?"

"There's another thing. When I... when I was with Thijs Falconer, he was talkin' about the case and how his dad had said he might get five years. Well he wouldn't've. No way. It was as though his dad was tryin' to frighten him into sayin' nuthin'. He said sumthin' about his dad puttin' the black on us for himself. At the time, I thought the lad meant that his dad was ensurin' that he stayed out of jail so that he could keep havin' his fun with him. Or so that there wouldn't be any abuse investigations. Now I'm thinkin' there may be more to it than that."

"In case something else might crop up that he wanted to keep hidden? These possible dodgy dealings? Yes, it's possible, I suppose. What about these media scandals that have been rocking soccer lately? Money in off-shore accounts and the like? Image rights?"

"I doubt it. Again, Ormerley are just a little team. It has to be sumthin' little, but big enough, if that makes sense. There's sumthin' I keep gettin' near," said Angells, frowning. "Sumthin' that happened some time back, but I can't seem to get a handle on it."

"Well, don't wake me at three in the morning shouting 'Eureka' when the penny's dropped."

"Unlikely. I'm no Galileo."

Should I tell him it was Archimedes? Ross wondered. Compared to what's been happening, and on a scale of importance from one to a hundred, it wouldn't even rate a nano-fraction. Instead he said, "Let's go to bed. You'll think better after a good night's sleep." Not that he expected his partner to have one.

* * *

The following evening, Angells was seated on the sofa, a pen drive and a manila folder on his knee.

"Every single thing we've got at the station on John Coverham," he said, answering the query arched on Ross's eyebrows, "and everythin' else I could dig up about him on the net. I was goin' screw-eyed starin' at the bloody computer screen, so I ended up printin' stuff. There has to be sumthin' in this lot, and to hell with any data-protection issues about bringin' stuff home."

"But, presumably, you've read it all before. From what I hear, it's not like you to miss anything."

"Oh?" Angells smiled at the compliment. "Who've you been talkin' to then?" he asked but didn't wait for an answer. "The stuff I dug out myself's new, and anyway, I was readin' with a different purpose in mind first time around."

Ross nodded and returned to his more prosaic paperwork. Occasionally resting his eyes and glancing up, he could almost see his partner's brain at work. Angells was methodical. He would read a page or so, then, still holding the sheet of paper as though doing so might make what he wanted jump off the page and hit him, he would stare into the middle distance, turning the words over in his mind, searching for a match with that flicker of a memory he had referred to the previous night. Dispensed with, the sheet would be neatly added to the growing pile at his side. Then, in the middle of the evening, when Ross was texting exhibitors lined up for a future show and Angells was two-thirds through his pile of information, he suddenly said, "Shit!" and hurriedly stood up.

Ross peered at him. "Are you issuing a command, an expletive or a dire warning?" he asked.

"The middle one!" said Angells, going to the table and picking up his laptop. "I've just remembered what that scam I was thinkin' of was. I bet it's on here somewhere."

When Angells had finished explaining, Ross said, "That's interesting, but would it put your man behind bars?"

"Yes, I think so. If these others are anythin' to go by, then yes, I think it would," he said.

Earlier that evening, Angells had been reading a selection of online extracts from the handbook issued by the EFL, the English Football League. It was clear that, although the EFL was self-governing, where a player had a written contract, a copy had to be lodged with both the EFL itself and with the Football Association at their London headquarters. Then, just prior to Mike's Archimedes moment, he had read a report printed in the local paper two years ago. John Coverham had just signed for Ormerley and so had four other players. What had caught Angells' eye was the fact that all five men had higher league experience and all were therefore used to much larger wages than a little League Two club like Ormerley could offer. There were pictures of the five signing their contracts with grins so broad and toothy that a reader might think they were signing for a big Premiership club with a Premier-sized salary to match.

Angells vaguely remembered an income tax fraud that had scandalised football at the time. He Googled some likely key words—and the details were there before him. Malverden Wanderers, a little south-east team who wanted to mix it with the big boys. The case had come to court in 2010.

What if, similar to then, there were two contracts, an official, League typical one for the EFL and FA—and therefore, of course, for the taxman, and a second, unofficial contract that guaranteed a lot more money? In other words, a system of bogus or parallel contracts designed to deceive a third party.

"I mean, it's obvious in a way," Angells explained. "Championship clubs want to be Premiership clubs. League clubs want to be Championship clubs. In fact, they've often been in the Championship but been relegated. But good players don't want to play in the lower leagues: they don't want the lower wages, they don't want to travel miles to play in some town they've never heard of in front of forty people, they don't want to shower in some changin' rooms that'd make a group of school kids play hooky on PE day. But if the clubs can inflate the players' wages artificially, illegally, if they find ways to dodge the taxman, they can encourage these better players to join the team."

"Too fast," said Ross. "You're losing me. You mean that tax is paid on the contract that's sent to the EFL and FA. That's all above board and legit."

"Yes."

"But there's another contract that they don't see. Offering far bigger salaries and, presumably, other under-the-table payouts, and because nothing is declared, no tax gets paid."

"Bang on. None of these extras are on the official contract sent to the EFL and FA, and therefore no tax is paid on them."

"OK. That makes sense. But how could a club finance it? Where would the money come from?"

"If you were lucky," Angells said, "you'd only have to find the finance for the first year. Then it'd pay for itself. Look… Ormerley got better players. Five of 'em. Much better ones than the other squads in League Two. They topped League Two easily and they won promotion directly—no need for play-offs—so they'd bank the greater gate receipts you get from playin' in League One, where the clubs are better supported. More matches would be televised, so they'd get bigger TV fees. Sky Sports. Channel 5. I haven't checked the amounts yet, but I bet it'd be thousands. If they did well in the FA Cup and the EFL Cup, that'd bring in thousands too, especially in the FA Cup if they drew the big clubs. Let's see…"

He hit a few more keys.

"Oh, God, I remember that. They reached the fifth round and drew City. The station was full of black and purple scarves! We'd nowhere to put 'em all!"

"You should have strung them up."

"That's a bit harsh for drunk and disorderly, isn't it?!"

"I meant the scarves, you idiot."

"I know you did."

"I suppose they could also fiddle the running expenses," said Ross, a trifle hesitantly.

Angells caught the hesitation.

"I'm not a detective for nuthin', you know," he said, studying Ross with suspicion. "You haven't been playin' naughty buggers, have you?"

Ross flushed and avoided his look but, realising that honesty might be a better policy than trying to hoodwink a CID inspector, said, "Well, they could have had building works and exaggerated the amount spent on ground improvements. Or even declared bogus building works."

"That what you did when we bought up the whole of Tunhead, is it?" said Angells, his face serious.

"Here, no. I wouldn't have dared with you looking over my shoulder! But I did do *something* like that when I had the gallery premises in Gateshead refurbished. Before I knew you! I could claim it on business expenses, you see. And the taxman gets so much. And I work so hard for so little. Are you very angry with me?"

Angells looked at him. "You'll find out later," he said enigmatically. "For now, let's get back to David Falconer. In that first year, before all that

TV money and stuff's coming in, it would be a way forward, yes—especially as they'd have to upgrade their ground and facilities to match those of the competition. It'd all seem very legit. So Falconer switches cash round. Takes money from A to pay for B. Like you said, claims for bogus buildin' works and such."

"Oh!"

"Oh what?"

"Well, I wouldn't say, only I know how important this is. You're not going to be too angry with me, are you, not when I'm trying to be helpful?"

"Out with it," growled Angells.

"Obviously I do a great deal of travelling in my profession and stay overnight in hotels…"

"Yes…?"

"On occasions, on exceedingly rare occasions you understand, I *might* have claimed some considerable expenses I didn't have." Ross met Angells' stony stare with a shy one of his own.

"*Might* have? You *might* have taken a risk, then. *If* you'd done it, of course," Angells said eventually. "If the taxman had wanted to see these *might*-be invoices and receipts, you'd have been for it. No *might* about it."

"Mike, we're surrounded by artists and people who would have gladly printed and published duplicates that weren't exactly duplicates."

"Stop! For God's sake, you're forgettin' I'm still a cop! What were you going to say, anyway?"

"Only that one could use the money saved from bogus building works or hotel accommodation to finance the initial extra payments and there might be other, similar means of switching money. Falconer would know, wouldn't he? And he'd do the covering up. I can think of a lot of ways to use this money. Loans—for that posh car for instance—ex-gratia payments, extra bonuses… and, as the club's accountant, he'd have to be privy to the dodgy dealings. He's the one who has to cook the books. Enough to see him behind bars though?"

"Well, in the case I've been lookin' through, the accountant got a fine and a suspended, but it seems she was little more than a fancy bookkeeper and, maybe, pressed on by some of the management. Falconer's the real McCoy, letters after his name and a professional council to answer to. I'll make a couple of enquiries to mates in the Fraud Squad. If they think there's a strong chance that a chartered accountant would get sent down, even for a short stretch, then I'll make it my business to send him."

"But why not get your mates in the Fraud Squad to do the whole thing? Why become involved yourself?"

Angells looked thoughtful for a minute.

"No," he said. "It has to be me, and me on my own. One: at the moment, I've not got enough proof. Fraud Squad won't act on a hunch. Two: it'd drag on too long. One of their many cases, and to be honest, Ross, every day's a day too long at the moment. I go into the station and live a lie. At least if I do it myself, I'll feel I'm tryin' to leave, if that makes sense—given, in a way, leavin's the last thing I want to do. *Does* that make sense? You know how bad I feel about deceivin' everyone."

"It makes sense. Yes," said Ross sympathetically.

"Three: if other cops at my station got involved, *my* involvement might get back to Falconer and, if that happens, who knows what he'd do or say? All this awful mess might end up bein' for nuthin'.

And four: it's personal. Very personal. I've only ever felt *as* personal as this about a case once before. I want to see this shiter put away. He mustn't know it's me, but *I* want to know it's me."

There was a silence while Ross considered not just his partner's words, but also the controlled ferocity they were spoken with. It gave birth to a thought that had crossed his mind before: he lived with a gentle but dangerous man.

It was very true. If Mike Angells was an angel, he was an avenging one.

"He's like a stick of Blackpool rock," Ross would sometimes explain to his friends. *"Deliciously sweet on the outside—you'd definitely want to take a few sticks home—but lick the sugar off and the centre's not so tasty."*

Mike Angells was, essentially, the same way he'd always been—kind, generous, lively, comfortable with himself and easy with others—but circumstances nurture layers on the inside, and at the centre of his psyche was a bitterness. It surfaced in a single way: the way he felt about punishment.

Collingwood, the bastard who'd mown down Sam, had had a fine, lost his licence and received six months, suspended. Had he been sent down for life, Mike still wouldn't have felt that justice had been done, not unless Collingwood *felt* his guilt every night, and often in the day. Sergeant O'Neill's passed-on message had gladdened his heart: Collingwood did feel guilt. However, if sending a man or woman to jail was the only way to provide an opportunity for that person to feel remorse, Angells would do everything legal to put them there. He was a man with empathy and sensitivity, and he by no means wished such mental torture on everyone he collared, but there were occasions, and this was one of them, when the bitterness surfaced and the harsh core, which was usually hidden, emerged.

Ross broke the silence. "OK. Let's make a scam like that the hypothesis. He's got to keep some covert record of his dodgy dealings because he has to make the books balance. How would you do it?"

"Make notes."

"Yes. How? On paper?"

"No. Paper leaves traces. Probably on Notepad if all I wanted was a load of simple text files. Bet he's pretty savvy. He'd want to cover his tracks, wouldn't he? Not leave any record lyin' round when he'd finished."

"Mm. So he'd delete everything, you think?"

"I wouldn't if it was me."

"Why not?"

"Well, deletin' files hides them from the user, but they're still there. They can be recovered, but it could take someone like me ages. There's some at the station who can do that sort of thing right fast—it's their job—but I can hardly commandeer his hardware while I try."

"So how would you go about covering your tracks?"

"If it was me, I'd overwrite the files. Grab some random text from an online newspaper or sumthin' and overwrite anythin' I didn't want somebody else to see."

"Can you still get the originals back?"

"All depends. It's a long shot."

"What's a long shot?"

Angells didn't answer. He was frowning, apparently at the light switch.

"Mike! Mike! Are you like this at work?"

"Like what?"

"Miles away. No wonder that crime stats are up for the first time for years!"

"Sorry, luv. And anyway, it's only some sorts of stats that are up *and* it's partly because of changin' the way crimes are recorded," he said defensively. "I was workin' it through. If he's used Notepad, which is what I'd do just for notes, there's a chance that each original file'd be small, say, under nine hundred bytes. Word files are much larger. Small files get some protection from overwritin', so they could still be there on the disc, probably with some easily recognisable file name: Foot1.txt, Foot2.txt—that sort of thing. I might get lucky."

"Worth a try?"

"Has to be. If it's the only lead you've got, you follow it even if the odds are long."

"No wonder people don't have much confidence in the police! That's how crimes are solved, is it? A guess and long odds."

"Cheeky! But sometimes it is. We can't all be Sherlock Holmes and Poirot, you know."

"Just as well. Can't stand scratchy violins, and I like a good brew, not a tisane," said Ross.

"Me neither, and me too. But it's true, lucky guesses some of the time. Or maybe that's doin' ourselves down. Not so much lucky guesses as instinctive ones. You get a feel for things."

"And is your feel for things telling you anything about David Falconer?"

"I think he's smart. I mean, if we're right and he's been runnin' this little op all this time, he's got to be smart, and if he's smart, he'll know he's better overwritin' than deletin'. But I still might get lucky if some of the files are small."

"So what will you do?"

"Well, I'll have to break into his office, won't I?" So he did.

* * *

Angells drove to Dansett Cross, where he knew David Coverham was based. He'd done his background checks. He knew that a ground-floor general reception cum switchboard area served all the offices in the building and that David Falconer's own suite overlooked the street on the third floor. The corridor opened onto Falconer's secretary's office. Then there'd be Coverham's own.

He also knew that the Falconer offices would be closed as it was the day of Thijs's funeral. He was surprised that he didn't find his choice of day distasteful. On the contrary, he felt it was right and proper to start to put the knife in then.

He gave his name and title to one of the young women on reception, Paula, and showed her his ID. His pretext was an official visit to a software house whose IT department was on the fourth floor. That much was true: he did have an appointment there, and he did pop his head in. He just took a little longer than was necessary to pop out of the building completely.

Getting into the secretary's office was easy enough for a man with his experience of picking locks. He ignored the secretary's computer and went straight to Falconer's in the room beyond. Chances were that the files he needed had been typed on that. He hoped so, anyway. He'd need a little luck!

He checked the things he needed and took what he called the scenic route back downstairs.

"Hello, Paula," he said when he reached reception again. He put on what Raith called his encouraging-serious face. "I noticed one or two potential security problems on my way up. Better safe than sorry. If you'll fill me in on a few details, I can send in a report and maybe someone'll act on it."

No problem. She was happy to oblige.

"Who handles your security?" he asked as they made their way upstairs.

It was Blacks in Bishop.

"Ah. I know of them," he said. He ought to. He used to pass the building they were housed in every day on his way to school. "Linked into their switchboard, is it?"

No, it wasn't—just internal. The last person out set the alarm. The alarm was by the main door.

"There's not a lot to steal." She laughed.

He laughed too. "Aye," he said noncommittally. "The alarm. Numerical, is it? Not one of those silly ones like 1234?"

"Oh no," said Paula. "3976."

He could get in from the front if necessary, but it was in full view of passing traffic. It would be risky. He'd noticed the infrared sensors by the ground and first floor windows.

"Are all your windows wired in to the system?" he asked Paula.

She thought so, but she wasn't sure about the ladies' toilet on the first floor—she'd never really looked—and she didn't know about the gents either. He'd already checked the gents. The window was too small for him to squeeze through.

Would she mind walking to the ladies with him and standing guard while he checked? He wouldn't want to surprise anyone.

The window was larger than the one in the gents, and it was open. No infrared detector. He looked out. It opened onto the side of the building, down an alley. It didn't look to be an easy climb, but he'd go round and check for hand and footholds when he left. He unscrewed the handle on the window and let it drop so that it would appear closed to anyone who stuck their head in at home-time.

"It looks fine, that," he said when he was back in the corridor. "What time do the offices get cleaned, Paula?" he asked as they returned to reception. The question had nothing to do with security, but he asked it so nonchalantly, in the midst of making general conversation about the rush hour trials of getting to work and traffic jams, that she didn't appear to notice any incongruity. Not till morning. Half past six.

"I suppose lots of people work late, though. Busy offices like this."

No. It wasn't that sort of place. Everyone was out by six as a rule. Couldn't wait to leave.

He thanked her for her help, and he was as good as his word—he sent in a report three days later. But by that time, he'd already broken in and got what he needed.

* * *

Angells headed back to Warbridge. However, he had one more task to complete before he could return to the station. He drove to a church cemetery on the west side of town and walked around until he came to the area reserved for recent burials. He found the plot he was searching for and read the card attached to David Falconer's wreath with disgust. 'Much loved son' indeed! The sod! He squatted down beside the newly laid turf.

"So I've got to put him somewhere where he'll have time to think, Thijs," he said aloud. "I won't just forget you or what he did to you. I will make him pay. I promise you, I'll see him sent down. I'll stay a cop until I do it. Then I'll leave. No more tears, heh?"

It suddenly occurred to him to wonder what he was talking to. He often went and knelt in Tunhead's little graveyard and talked to Sam. Nothing morbid. Just… talk. It was daft, but he did it and always felt a little better for doing so. He'd even told him he'd been back to Emelda's. But at least Sam was there, or his bones were there at least. Something was. What was underneath Thijs's patch of grass? What was left when someone went under a train? Abruptly, he stood up. He wished he could drive home. Instead he had three hours left of his shift.

* * *

Angells was glad that the nights were drawing in and providing at least a little cover of darkness. He collected his belongings, checking them off against the list he'd made: two pairs of gloves—one to make sure he didn't leave fingerprints, one to give him a grip on the windowsill—torch, lock-picks, mobile, drink, blackout sheet, pen drive… and before wheeling his bike round to the path, he added two large blocks of stone from the rockery in the garden.

He left the bike in a side road that wasn't covered by cameras and took a route to the office block that was also, to the best of his knowledge, surveillance free. There was a wheelie bin further down the alley at the building's side. He moved it underneath the toilet window then jammed it in place with the blocks of stone. He placed the backpack inside the bin, to be recovered later. Then, using the strength gained from working on rings and bars in one of Warbridge's gyms, he placed his hands on the bin and raised himself up onto it. He could just reach the windowsill when he stood up. He crouched, sprang and gained a grip. Then, levering himself up again, he pushed the window open and scrambled inside.

Even in the dark, he could visualise exactly the route to Falconer's office. He found his way there confidently. He played with the lock, went inside and drew the blinds. He hung the blackout sheet over them to minimise the glare from the computer screen, and switched on.

The request for a password. He hoped, how he hoped, it would be... yes, it was! Valkenier. He'd mentioned the word—the Falconers' house name—to Ross and suggested it was French. Ross had laughed, said, "Clever bugger," and added "It's Dutch. For Falconer." In the DI's considerable experience, people kept to a password they liked, especially if a little conceit was in the mix. He could imagine David Falconer feeling very self-satisfied choosing a translation of his name. Angells reckoned, correctly, that he'd use it repeatedly, wherever a password was needed.

He drew the chair closer to the desk.

* * *

At three o'clock in the morning, Ross was woken by sounds from the kitchen. If it was burglars, they were making a drink and whistling happily.

"Hello! I wasn't expecting you back for hours," he said when he'd gone downstairs.

"I wasn't expectin' to be back, luv, but I got it!" Angells took his pen drive out of his pocket and put it on the table. "I had a really lucky break," he said.

"Then make me a drink too," said Ross, unable

to resist adding, "now that you've got me up at this ridiculously unearthly hour, and tell me all about it."

"Well…" said Angells, and explained what he'd done.

He'd taken a look at the root folder. To his joy, he saw a group of text files, all written in Notepad, all the same length and all having similar file names—in this case, orm1.txt, orm2.txt and so on. He'd opened the first file. Raspberries. It was about growing raspberries. It started in mid-sentence and it stopped in mid-sentence too. The next one was about growing raspberries. In fact, it proved to be identical to the first. The third file, and the fourth, and the fifth all turned out to be the same. Raspberries.

Had Falconer done what he'd thought? Had he tried overwriting some important notes with text grabbed from an article on growing raspberries?

"I plugged in me drive and launched the disk editor to set up a search of the raw disk data, sector by sector," he explained. "A few minutes later, there it was: the filename. And below it, the player's name, and the evidence we wanted—proof of sumthin' dodgy in one little paragraph. I didn't know whether to sigh with relief or give the computer a kiss."

Of course, he'd done neither but made a copy of the sector data in a file on his drive. Then he went back to search for the next of the filenames.

"Tell you one thing," he said. "It was harder gettin' out of that bloody buildin' than it was gettin' into it. I fell off the bloody wheelie bin I'd stuck under the window. Banged me knee sumthin' awful."

"Poor thing," said Ross. "Burglary's evidently far too physically challenging for you. Finished your drink, by the way?"

Angells nodded.

"Then hobble upstairs and I'll kiss your knee better!"

"Me mouth hurts too," said Angells, climbing the stairs after him, "and me arms and me neck and me shoulder. In fact I hurt all over. There's not one bit of me that doesn't hurt…"

They fell into bed. Dawn was breaking before they went to sleep.

* * *

Raith

What Phil's said isn't exactly gospel truth. He makes it sound as if I had some "St Paul on the road to Damascus" epiphany or something, where the light switched on and I suddenly realised I was some brilliant Dali-type figure and gay to boot! Well, that would be surreal wouldn't it? Maybe Ken Price would be nearer the mark. I really like his ceramics. Thing is, Phil's as much St Mark as I'm St Paul. He wasn't there. He's picking things up from what's been said and making some sort of history about it. So, for example, when I got shut in that cattle shed of a prison, it wasn't quite like he said. It was fucking brutal, I know that much, and I was fucking scared but… not quite like he made it out to be, even though he says that's how I told it.

One thing he's got right, though. I do remember that day in the garden. Not just remember it either. Feel it and smell it and taste it as if it was happening right now. Feel the heat. It was hot that day, blistering hot, and even the birds had stopped singing, as if it was all too much effort—which was just as well as there'd been a group of sparrows going chirp-chirp-bloody-chirp, and if they hadn't shut up when they did, I'd have thrown my beer glass at them. Waste of a good pale ale (and, yes, Phil was drinking brown.)

There were lots of different smells. I don't mean flower smells. People smells. Angel Baby's delicious, sweaty Oxo-graviness that I could smell despite his splash of Lynx. Well I couldn't put the sounds and the smells on the picture and, for a different reason, I couldn't put all the things I saw in either. I didn't put the butterflies in. Heaps of the sodding things. They were everywhere. Painted ladies, Ross said. And when one of them landed on the back of Angel Baby's hand… you know what? That scared me more than being banged up with Ti and Joe did. I'm superstitious, I suppose. It's childhood stuff you can't get out of your head even when you're supposed to be grown up and a rational adult. My mam used to say (probably still does say) that a butterfly's the soul of someone good who's died. Well Angel Baby wasn't dead, but when that butterfly landed on him, it stayed put for ages till he moved his finger and it flew away. I just felt cold—in the blazing heat of that day. I got a shiver, the way you do when you open the freezer lid and you're blasted by cold air. And he saw me looking at him and he asked me if I was all right, all concerned and aware that something was bothering me, and I mumbled, "Yeah of course," thinking, *I am, but you're not,* and he wasn't all right. God help him, he wasn't all right, and as sure as I'm sitting here, I know that that sodding butterfly was trying to lay claim to him. I should have smashed the fucking thing to pulp and fed it to the sodding sparrows. Cos he wasn't all right, was he?

Chapter 14

Ross and Angells couldn't continue pooling their mental resources as quickly as they wanted to. It wasn't so much that they were busy, but rather that they wanted Raith to be well out of the way. Two evenings later, though, he'd gone to Warbridge to spend the night at Phil's.

"So, what have we got?" asked Ross as he and Mike sat beside each other on the sofa in their living room, currant buns and strong coffee within reach: they were expecting a lengthy session.

"Appreciate the 'we'," said Angells before recapping the list of salient points. "Fact one: Ormerley FC were promoted to League One at the start of this season.

"Fact two: five players joined them last season who'd had higher league experience.

"Fact three: John Coverham was one.

"Fact four: terms of his first Ormerly contract were very generous for League Two.

"Fact five: ditto his current League One contract. It has him gettin' nearly three thousand pounds per week plus bonuses. Over a hundred and fifty grand a year. That's twice the average of a League One salary."

"Oh? I thought that football players did well."

"Premiership and Championship. But it tails off fast. Accordin' to what I've been readin' online, average pay in the Championship for the 2014/15 season was over three hundred grand per year, but it dropped to seventy grand for League One and forty grand for League Two. So, even allowin' for the fact that this season's figures will be higher, a hundred and fifty grand is still way up on what you'd expect.

"Fact six: JC, in conversation with TF, implies that DF is involved in sumthin' shady."

"Is that a fact, Mike?"

"The most likely arrangement of the facts. Firm enough ground, I'd say, given the next thing we know… Fact seven: notes on DF's computer link payments made to five players with a disparate range of invoices."

He pointed to various examples on a table he was partway through drawing up.

"I've only had a chance to look through the Coverham file," he said. "I've not had a chance to look at the others. Here's a good example." Angells indicated a line reading *JC, 02.03.16/ £350 bonus*. Alongside it was *W. Dog, 25.02.16 £350+1700*. "My readin' of that is that, in March 2016, Coverham got an undeclared bonus of £350. It was covered up on the books by addin' £350 to a £1700 February hotel invoice, the White Dog maybe—there's a White Dog in Bishop.

"Here's another. Look." Angells pointed to a second entry made in March. It read *JC, 15.03.16 / £400 ex-g*. Then, alongside, *BN, S. Shields, 10.03.16 £800+7600. See PM*. "There's a landscapin' outfit in Shields, Brian Nichols. They do block pavin', hard landscapin' not gardens. Beckover and I recovered a whole load of their tools and equipment from the Hartlepool docks when we were on that farm machinery case. Small stuff—tampers, angle grinders, that sort of thing, but it all added up. What if this is them, and they invoice Ormerley for £7600 but Falconer puts it on the books as eight four? That gives him £800 to play around with. Four hundred to Coverham, ex-gratia. Four hundred to PM, who I guess is Pablo Mendez, one of the five we're interested in."

Ross was examining the rest of the table and noticing several similar entries.

"Yes, I agree with you," he said, "and, presumably, these initials here are shorthand for other hotels and for firms that have provided services. Electrics, building works etc. All local firms, I imagine."

"Probably local. Keeps your mates sweet and well-fed if you feed 'em work. Nuthin' to say they knew what was goin' on, though. The hotels could be anywhere. Ormerley play nationally, remember. It might be stay-overs for the players, or it could be executive weekends and the like."

"The sums here aren't huge, Mike."

"I know, but what you've got there is just for March and, with a couple of exceptions, just for Coverham. I guess Falconer doesn't want to draw attention to what's goin' on, so he's got to be a bit circumspect. There are five players and it all adds up."

"Yes, you're right, and this might only be a snapshot of what's happening. I presume, though," said Ross, "that you can't show the means by which he's diverted the cash to pay for all these top-ups to salary. The sums may be virtual but the payments are real. He has to get that three hundred and fifty and the eight hundred from somewhere."

"True. I don't know. As far as I can see, I've only got info about where the money goes to. Nuthin' about where it comes from. But it wouldn't matter, would it, if I can show that there are parallel contracts and mismatches between the genuine invoices and what it seems he's puttin' on the books? I'm used to bodies in the library, not a paper chase, but I'm pretty sure I'm right. If I can provide evidence of systematic abuse, then HMRC would be duty bound to follow it up, and they will have the resources to uncover the whole story."

"I imagine you're right, yes. You would just have to show that something irregular is happening regularly, with Falconer's knowledge and complicity, and they would do the rest. He's taking a risk, Mike. If the Tax wanted to check up on the original invoices and compare them to the books… As I told you, if I'd been asked, I'd have got someone here to print my own bills off."

Angells ignored one reference but commented on the other. "Aye, but that's how people get caught. They think they're so clever they can get away with anythin', so they don't see it as a risk. Not one they can't handle, anyway."

He forced aside the thought that, at that moment, swept into the very core of his being. He was taking a risk too, but at least he was aware of it. Well aware. The same thought had obviously occurred to Ross.

"You're taking a risk too, Mike," he said anxiously.

"No bigger than the one I've already taken," said Angells. "Come on, let's think ahead." He brusquely brushed aside Ross's concern and hoped he sounded a lot more confident than he felt.

"I need to see the original hotel and company invoices and the official contracts Ormerley sent to the FA or EFL. If we're right about the parallel contracts, there'll be a big discrepancy between the FA/EFL contract and the one I've seen and, whatever the difference is, that amount'll be tax free. Same with last year's contract. And the other four players—I need to see their contracts too. I haven't got their unofficial parallel contracts, assumin' such contracts exist, but there may be some things I can tie in with the info on the disk."

"Fine. Where are the headquarters? Do you have mates in the Met? With the FA HQ being in London..."

"Contacts in the Met—a few, yeah, but not so's I could involve them in this, and anyway, they'd need a pretext for seein' the stuff. The EFL's in Preston. The administration is, anyway. The commercial end's London too. I don't know which'd be easiest. I do know someone who might help, and seein' things he shouldn't see is right up his street. I'll get on to him."

"I can work through your table and transcribe the rest of the info from your drive too if you want."

"Really? Great, yeah. Have you got the time to do that, though?"

"Well, we might have to forego my wonderful cooking for the next few days, though I could always ask Raith to come home and toss up a meal or two."

"God help us, no! I need a clear belly as well as a clear head. I'm just goin' to phone a nice lad I met a few months ago," he added.

Ross looked miffed.

"Don't look jealous!"

"I'm not jealous. I just feel that I'm wasting my culinary skills living with you," said Ross sniffily.

It was difficult to feign confidence and carelessness, but Angells knew that he had to. Inside... inside he felt like jelly. If he were caught...

He was back in that layby, seeing a future full of blood and bruises, banged up, banged up—yes! His heart sometimes beat so strongly that he thought it would break free of his skin. Sheer terror.

But Ross had been really shaken up by what had happened too. Not initially. He'd been very defensive initially, but since then—the things he'd said, the things he'd done, the look Angells would catch on his face… Angells was adept at reading people. All good interviewers were. He knew he had to draw on every ounce of his own faltering strength to keep the two of them from folding, but in one way, the hardest task they faced was nothing to do with obtaining information, nor with finding evidence of Falconer's guilt. It was hiding this whole sordid, unwished-for business from Phil and Raith. It was a secret that had to be kept, for fear of implicating the other two men in a cover-up that could cause all four of them to finish up in jail.

So Mike strove to keep life in Tunhead light-hearted, and he forced himself to encourage the little verbal fencing matches he and Ross enjoyed. Sometimes, though, he didn't have to fake it; Ross's little comments genuinely made him smile.

He grinned at the last one and went to make his phone call.

The man he phoned was a spook called Dick Baxter who worked for a branch of the government anti-terrorism squad. He and his colleagues could get into all manner of places that were way beyond the reach of normal policemen—physical places and IT ones too. Mike had met Baxter the previous year when a threat to the Metro Centre had required much liaison. Baxter had been less secretive than his colleagues and had furnished Mike with useful information. *"I think he's a bi-*

guy," Mike had said by way of explaining the confidences to Flaxby. Being in the club did have one or two advantages then. So Angells had phoned Dick Baxter to see if he'd help him again.

Mike made his phone call on the Thursday evening. On Monday afternoon, he downloaded ten attachments from his computer. Baxter had wasted no time, and Angells simply e-mailed 'Thanks.' He had no need to print copies of the Coverham contracts he'd already seen. Each detail was etched on his memory, and as he'd hoped and—in truth—had expected, the content was markedly different from the contracts the club had registered officially. There was no mention of a loyalty bonus, nothing about a large signing-on fee. There was, however, thousands of pounds' difference in the annual salary, and hundreds of pounds' difference in what were deemed allowable expenses. It was obvious now that some folk at Ormerley were playing the parallel contracts game and equally obvious that Falconer was deeply involved in the covering up.

Angells felt pleased, surprising himself that he didn't feel any greater emotion. Just pleased, and cool and somehow detached. It was the feeling of a hunter who knew he was en route to catching his prey.

* * *

"Police work is very laborious," Ross complained to Angells that Monday evening. "I thought that playing cops and robbers would be much more fun."

"Playin', eh? Stop gripin'," was Angells' unsympathetic retort. He hardly took his eyes off the notes he was making.

"Yes, Inspector," said Ross with mock humility. "Anyway, here's my hard-earned contribution. I'm sorry it's taken so long. I used the Trades websites to hazard a guess at the firms indicated on Falconer's disk," he said. "Where I've included more than one entry, it's because I'm uncertain which of two, in one case three, firms the initials refer to. I thought it was interesting that so many different firms are used—as though they want to spread any dodgy dealings round."

Angells nodded his agreement as he read through the proffered list.

"It suggests the businesses aren't part of the set up," he said. "He'd've stayed with just a couple of tried and trusted ones if he'd wanted them involved."

"Also, I did what you suggested and checked the venues Ormerley played at against hotels in the area. The home games too. The internet made such investigation relatively easy."

Angells took the hotel print-out.

"This is great, Ross," he said. "You really have put a lot of work in. I can see that."

"Thank you. There's something else," said Ross. "This hotel—" He pointed to two entries that possibly referred to a hotel in Tunhope. "This is the one Alison works in."

Alison was the daughter of a wrought-iron worker whose workshop was in BOTWAC.

"It is, yes," said Angells. "Are you thinkin' that she might be able to help us see the books? She's a waitress there, though. She might not be able to access to the books without lookin' snoopy. I wouldn't want to put her in a compromisin' position."

"Me neither, of course, but perhaps she could get a look at the hotel register for the dates in question and at least see how many rooms were booked, et cetera. For the whole team? The management? Friends of? We can check the prices ourselves. And I'm sure if you asked nicely, she'd help you see more. But there's this one too," Ross added, brandishing a piece of paper. "I'm sure this is The Collier's, a few miles south of Gateshead. Whenever I've important visitors and artists for shows in Newcastle or Gateshead itself, I use this hotel. I'm sure they'd help as a personal favour. Eleven entries. Look at this one…"

He pointed to one entry of several thousand pounds.

"Perhaps this refers to one of those pre-season training sessions that one hears of. Bonding exercises."

Angells nodded. "You deserve a chocolate biscuit for all that," he said.

"Is that all?"

"Two then."

"Don't I get a sheriff's star? Seeing as I've been seconded to the police, that is."

"I'll make you one out of cooking foil. How's that? These here are interesting," Mike said, refocusing on the list. He pointed to well over a dozen other entries that involved north-east hotels and businesses that lay outside his own division's remit. "These fall in Beckover's patch. Remember him? The farm op?"

"Of course. Not likely to forget, am I? Great to gaze at the stars, but not at three in the morning when your balls are turning to ice."

Angells grinned. "Sorry. I bet he'd help, though, and he wouldn't ask too many questions. He owes me."

"Mike," Ross asked, halfway through his third biscuit, "we've sort of got A, B and C, but what we've got doesn't take us to Z, does it? I mean, what about the other original invoices?"

"I've been thinkin' on it," said Angells. "Ten of the firms you reckon are in Falconer's notes are ones that I had dealin's with after the farm affair. As well as the small stuff I told you about, the equipment belongin' to Brian Nichols, we recovered a load of high-end construction equipment: fork lifts, JCBs, Manitous, telehandlers. Big expensive stuff. I can go back to all these firms myself and ask to see the invoices. I'm still on those cases, and we're still tryin' to match some stuff up with the owners so… all true."

Ross nodded. "So, we'll be able to show that the dodgy dealing is systematic—all ten contracts, not just one—and we'll have information about invoices that the taxman can check against Falconer's books should they feel there's a case to answer. Surely that would be enough for them to act upon and begin their own investigations?"

"Yes, it would. I checked with one of the guys from Fraud Squad. Without sayin' why, obviously. I asked him who to send information to as well. I don't want it just to end up at the bottom of someone's pile, never seein' the light of day, and I don't want it to go to someone who'll just dismiss it as small fry."

"So, what next?"

"Bed, I think. I'm knackered."

* * *

It took another four weeks for Angells to prepare a sufficiently detailed and damaging dossier to send to an investigator at the large HMRC department in Newcastle. The dossier itself was unsigned.

It actually proved easier to retrieve information

than Angells had originally thought it would. The management at the Gateshead Collier's would have drowned him in data had he not said, gratefully, "Enough!" He didn't even need to contact the village lass who worked at the hotel in Tunhope, for, more fruitfully, he reaped the rewards of the efforts he'd made earlier that year when working on the Tun Beck farm machinery op.

The management of the construction firms he'd been in contact with over the recovered equipment were only too glad to provide him with copies of their invoices. The grateful *Inspector* Beckover had come good and hadn't asked him any questions he couldn't answer truthfully. Angells told Beckover that the Coverham case— still open, of course—had loose ends that needed tying together and that details about Ormerley-related invoices formed a necessary part of that investigation. Beckover's input was especially useful, for it widened the scope, geographically, of the inquiries. Angells' only real concern was ensuring that Beckover contacted him direct. He didn't want anyone at the Warbridge station receiving calls or information meant for his ears only, but stressing the need for such secrecy might—probably *would*—cause a naturally suspicious cop to be even more suspicious, and he didn't want to involve his colleague any more than necessary. So he made his requests for personal communication as nonchalantly as possible, hopeful that his face would betray no anxiety and that his voice would betray none either.

There was, however, one person based at Warbridge whom he couldn't completely fool.

"What's the inspector always hiding behind his door for?" asked Fortune of Superintendent

Flaxby one morning. "Can't be to look at porn in private, not with all the fun and games that must go on up Tun Beck."

Flaxby didn't answer, partly because he'd decided that the best way to deal with Fortune's lascivious comments was to treat them with the distance they deserved, partly because he'd wondered the same thing himself—albeit without the Tunhead reference—and partly, mainly, because of the folder he held in his hand. Finally, he said, almost to himself, "I want to see him when he gets in."

"When you see him! If you see him!" said Fortune, and returned to his own office to sulk and fletch more arrows.

Through his open window, Flaxby heard the sound of Angells' bike. He shouted down to the car park to tell Angells that he wanted to see him. When the inspector arrived, Flaxby studied him for several seconds and then, waving the folder, explained.

"This," he said with dangerous emphasis, "is a copy of a report that found its way to me unofficially by a circuitous route from someone who remembered that one of our many unsolved cases involves a dead footballer called John Coverham and an equally dead suspect called Thijs Falconer. Now there's a coincidence, given that you, Inspector, have been so involved in that case."

He paused. Angells said nothing.

"And here's a surprise. It seems that Falconer's father is going to find himself the subject of an investigation, though not, apparently, one of ours. The son didn't get sent down, but the father probably will. And this…" he said, offering the folder to Angells. Angells saw what Flaxby was holding and was visibly shocked. "…is what's led to that investigation. Not only that, but there's only one person I know who itemises reports in this idiosyncratic way, and that person is you. So, Inspector," said Flaxby malevolently, "tell me when it was I seconded you to Fraud Division."

Angells stared at the folder. He hadn't expected to see it held in Flaxby's hands.

"Concise, precise, itemised in your inimitable manner… It *was* you, wasn't it?"

"Yes, sir," Angells managed to say.

"Well if you're expecting compliments for a job well done, you've come to the wrong bloody place. What the bloody hell were you playing at? Under my nose? I'd no bloody idea what was going on!"

"I'll tell you, sir—"

"Yes, you bloody will!"

"—but not here. Not now. There's things I'll have to do—"

"WHAT?!"

"Things I'll have to do. Then, please can I come and talk to you? Privately?"

"Privately? What are you planning to confess? That you're transgender or a transvestite and you're really a woman in disguise?"

As soon as Flaxby said that, he felt ashamed. It was the kind of cheap comment that Fortune might make. The realisation calmed him down, though he didn't apologise.

"What time do you finish?" he asked.

"Six, sir. Sir, don't tell anybody I wrote this report, please, not till you've heard me out, and not even then," Angells pleaded. The man looked distraught.

"My place. Six fifteen sharp. I'll give you half an hour."

"Thank you."

"Now get out of my sight and keep out of it till then."

Angells didn't need telling twice. He shot out of the room.

This was it, then. He'd done all he could.

He'd heard little about his dossier since Phil had delivered it, in person, to the Newcastle office. He'd explained why he didn't want to go himself and told Phil enough of the background for Phil to be a willing ally. He couldn't divulge everything. Phil would have become implicated had he done so. He'd known that Flaxby would get to know about the dossier—it involved a criminal on his patch—but Angells knew he'd concealed his own identity so, as far as he could see, there was no reason for him to admit involvement. To find that not only had things moved faster than he'd expected—indeed, as fast as he'd hoped—but that he had been sussed, and because of the way he wrote his reports…

He looked around his little room. This time, there'd be no dead bodies to stop him handing in his resignation. This time, there'd be no last-minute visits to the stationery cupboard; he'd ensured he had a stock of envelopes. He printed his resignation letter out and put it in an envelope addressed to Chief Constable Mayfield. He would put it on the CC's desk just before he left. Left for good. He still hadn't taken the holidays he was owed, and so he wouldn't have to work his notice period.

It all seemed a bit of an anti-climax really. Was it worth trying to focus on the cases he'd been working on? He tried to but found he just thought about the people he'd be leaving behind. He knew he would be leaving them behind completely. If you retired, you left folk behind, but if you came across them socially, you could still talk to them. Be pleased to see them. Chat about mutual colleagues. Reminisce. Not after what *he'd* done, though. This was cutting himself off forever.

He'd miss Flaxby. In his way, he had a great deal of love for Flaxby. The super had always supported him. He knew he was Flaxby's favourite, and he knew how much Flaxby would be hurt by the revelations he would hear that evening. He understood the super's anger at being kept in the dark. How would Flaxby react when he told him the fuller story? He knew that, now, he'd have to. He'd betrayed the super's trust.

Well, you never know what you're capable of until you're tested. You never know what you care about until you're faced with losing it. Small comfort, though.

Only four o'clock. He could always rehearse what he intended to say, he supposed. Rehearsals had never seemed necessary, though. He knew people who did go through their lines as though practising a play so that when they delivered them in a briefing they'd be word perfect. Angells couldn't understand the need. You start in the right place. You continue. Easy as that. But what was the right place? Not with what Ross did. He'd have to skate over that and bank on the fact that the super would have no interest in dragging up a cold case involving Ross when he was staring at a fresh one involving his beloved division.

Was he banking on that too? That Flaxby would let himself be party to a cover up in order to protect not Angells himself but everyone else? In all honesty, it hadn't been an issue, and it had played no part whatsoever in deciding his actions. He'd done what he felt he'd had to, and he'd been willing to risk the consequences. All of them.

Well, this mess he was in had started with Coverham's death, so Coverham's death was the place to start.

And so the hours dragged slowly by. He could almost hear the seconds ticking. Finally, six o'clock came. His office was tidy. Nothing out of place. He forced himself to leave it without a backward glance, to leave the CID floor without a backward glance, to leave the building without a backward glance. He unchained his bike and, without the roaring revs that usually signalled his departure, he left the station car park for the final time.

It was nearly November and the clocks had changed, so it was dark as he rode to Flaxby's house. He climbed off his bike and, at six fifteen precisely, he rang the bell on the super's door.

"Shut the door behind you," said Flaxby. He turned his back on Angells and went into the living room.

Angells deposited his crash helmet on the little table in the hallway, followed the super into the room and sat down on the edge of the chair indicated. Flaxby pointed to the report. It lay upon a coffee table.

"When did you join the Fraud Squad then?" he asked sarcastically. "Remind me, did I suggest a transfer there?"

There weren't really any useful answers to either question, so Angells said nothing.

"So what's going on? *Something's* been going on. Well come on, Mike. Stop gulping in air like a bloody beached whale. I haven't got all night."

Angells hadn't realised how heavily he was breathing. *And I haven't even started yet,* he thought.

Eventually, and after some forced, slow, deep breaths, he said, "I've resigned, sir."

"Bloody hell!" said Flaxby. It felt like he'd just received confirmation of a bad diagnosis—the news was half-expected, but still shocking. No... On the other hand, he hadn't expected it at all, even though he'd known that something was amiss. Shit. Angells. Leaving. "Why?"

This was what Angells had been dreading. Confessing. Explaining. *Come on*, he thought. *Which is harder and more painful? Telling Flaxby what you are or telling the truth to yourself?* And armed with the knowledge that this was far easier, he took a breath and began.

"The Coverham case," he said. "Thijs Falconer was involved in John Coverham's death. He pushed him. Coverham fell and cracked his head.

"Years ago, Ross—my Ross that is—did sumthin' really stupid. David Falconer, Thijs Falconer's dad, knew about it. He put the black on me. To protect Ross, I withheld evidence. I misrepresented evidence. I knowingly assisted Thijs Falconer to fabricate a statement and... deceive everyone."

To his amazement, he'd found he could make most of the confessions fairly smoothly. That one though, to actually admit deception, he'd found very, very hard.

He continued. "I neglected to do my duty. I've been guilty of gross misconduct. I knew from the start I'd have to resign. Thijs Falconer wanted me to get hold of some videos of him and Coverham that were hidden at Coverham's house. I did. The stuff on them was..." He paused again. "They were horrible. I could see why the lad was so screwed up. His dad was a monster. I thought of usin' the stuff I saw—confront the dad with it—but my hands were already tied. I'd already said I'd do what he wanted, and I'd already sat on evidence.

Anyway, he'd've known I was bluffin' cos if he'd called it, then Ross would've been exposed. He'd've made sure of that. Revenge. So it was already too late. He'd know I wasn't prepared to risk exposin' Ross.

"The day Thijs Falconer died, I went back to his house to give him the videos. I went in part to talk to him. To try to make him see that if he… that he… to tell him he couldn't let those things happen, that he had to try and get some help. He was so scared and so vulnerable."

Angells stopped. He closed his eyes as the memory of that day came back to him. He got no help from Flaxby. None at all. Not even sarcasm. He took another deep breath, sighed and began again.

"You can hear what we said. I'd wired up. I've brought a copy for you. I didn't want to leave it on your desk, obviously. You can hear it all. *Nearly* all. You can even hear us fuckin' if you want."

He pulled the little cassette out of his pocket and laid it on top of the folder. Then there was another, longer pause as he fought for the composure to continue. And still, not an ounce of help from Flaxby.

"He asked me to stay or to see him again. I told him no, I couldn't. I was a cop. I had Ross."

Angells sharply sucked in a breath, not least because he was aware that Flaxby had greeted the statement "I was a cop" with a grunt of derision.

"I came back to the station. I printed off my resignation. I'd already put it on file. I signed it, dated it and realised I hadn't any envelopes. I went to the stationery cupboard and I had the letter in my hand, and you called me into your office and said he was dead, under a fuckin' train. I knew I couldn't handle it and so I turned away, pushed my fingers down my throat and spewed up so you wouldn't know why I was shakin' like a jelly and so you wouldn't see the letter—I reckoned you wouldn't want to see sumthin' covered in honk. Cos right then, I knew I couldn't resign. First thing, I knew there'd be an inquiry and if I resigned it'd be suspicious. Second thing… somehow, I had to make his fuckin' shithole of a dad pay. I would've killed him if he'd been stood there in front of me. I'd've thumped him till I'd broken every bone in his body, until he was in as many pieces as his son must've been under that train and I still wouldn't've stopped. It's not enough. Gettin' him on a tax fraud's not enough, but it's sumthin'. If it gets him banged up for just a little while, that's sumthin'. At least he'll lose his job and maybe have time to think. And that's what I want him to have. Time to sit in a cell and think about all the pain he's caused to his own child, his own lad, and maybe feel some of that pain himself."

There was silence.

"So," said Flaxby eventually, "anything else you'd like to confess while we're here?"

Angells said nothing.

"And just what are you after? Compliments for single-handedly bringing a criminal to justice?"

"No. Of course not."

"Just as well, cos you won't get them from me, Angells. Were you so bloody confident in your detecting skills that it never occurred to you to think what might have happened if this little game you were playing had come to light? I take it you weren't bothered that you've let everyone waste time looking for someone to hang Coverham's death on. Or that you could've put Topley and Sanghera through a fucking ordeal. What a fucking hypocrite you've been. What kind of example were you showing them—all those lads and lasses in CID? You bastard, Angells. You've let them down. You evil bastard."

Again, Angells said nothing. He didn't need to be told. He knew.

"Didn't you think what would happen to you? If you got sent down for being bent?"

"Of course I did! Night after night after night, I did. Wakin' up screamin' and sweatin' and out of my mind with fear and worry. Of course I did! And every dream the same: every lag I've ever helped put away rapin' me and fuckin' me and stretchin' me so wide with whatever they found lyin' around you'd get a bus up my ass. Then stringin' me up and kickin' away the chair. Watchin' me dance on the end of a rope with my balls shoved in my mouth… Of course I was scared."

Angells stood up and turned away. He buried his head in his hands as if in hope that shutting out the light would shut out his imagination.

"You deserve to be scared," said Flaxby contemptuously. "You broke every rule in the book. And now you're what? Telling me this, hoping I won't turn you in? For old times' sake or something? Is that what you think?"

The punch Angells felt in the small of his back sent him sprawling to the floor. He heard rather than felt a rib crack as Flaxby kicked hard and, kicking again, flipped him onto his back. Then another vicious kick in the ribs.

"Clive! Stop! Please!" begged Angells as more heavy kicks rained down.

"Don't fucking call me Clive. You lost the right to call me Clive when you put my division at risk, you bastard," said Flaxby. He looked more furious than Angells had ever seen him.

Flaxby grabbed Angells' arm, dragged him

off the floor and slammed him onto the chair. He punched Angells' face hard, and hard again, and again.

"That one's for Sanghera. And that's for Topley. And that one's for Ron Fortune because, God help me, he's been right about you. Two of the bloody things for Fortune."

Christ, that was close to his eye. Angells knew he should be parrying the blows and trying to defend himself, but he didn't even try. One final thump, harder than any of the others and right on his mouth.

"And that one's for me."

Angells wiped his bust lips with the back of his hand and ran his tongue against a jagged tooth edge. Broken. God knows where the rest of the tooth was. Not in his mouth. That was full of blood and red spittle. He knew he should take deep, steady breaths, but the pain in his ribs and his kidneys meant that only shallow, ragged ones were possible.

Flaxby was looking at him, full of contempt.

"The one thing you've done right—the *one* thing—is you've handed your notice in. The Force doesn't need a shite like you. And the only reason I'm not turning you in right now is to protect everyone else, but I reckon you were banking on my doing that. So fuck off back to Tunhead and Whitburn, whatever he's done, and the rest of your damn band of lovers. I don't even want to know what Whitburn did. The two of you deserve each other. I don't ever want to see your face again. Fucking ever. You're despicable. Now get out of my house."

Angells stood up shakily but had to clutch Flaxby for support. The super shook him off and pushed him out of the room. He shoved him down the hall, opened the front door and pushed him through, throwing Angells' crash helmet after him.

"Fuck off!" he shouted, and slammed the door shut.

Angells picked up his helmet and managed to stagger to his bike, but he knew he was in no state to ride. He knelt on the ground and leaned against the back wheel. He didn't need two fingers in his mouth this time. Trembling, he retched and retched and spewed up everything he'd eaten and drunk that day. It felt like everything he'd downed that week. Fear, relief, pain. He didn't know which made the greatest contribution. Finally, after what seemed an age but in fact was only a few minutes, he began the journey home.

* * *

Angells had no idea how he reached Tunhead that evening. A week later, when he could ease his bruised and battered body down the narrow terrace stairs, venture outdoors and take a look at his bike, he could see that he'd run into a hedge. Judging by the many spiny sprigs of hawthorn attached to both mudguards, it had been a fair old smash. He sucked in his breath. He could have hit a wall. He didn't remember crashing, though. He didn't remember much of the last few days, really. Just snatches.

He knew that there'd been people around. He had some recollection of trying, unsuccessfully, to push them away when they'd bathed and bandaged him. He knew that, every so often, someone had squirted a phial of something bitter-tasting between his busted lips and that he'd, briefly, struggled against the weariness that had then flooded over him. And he knew that there'd been soup. Gallons of tomato soup. He felt he was drowning in tomato soup, but maybe it was just his own blood he was seeing and tasting. He didn't know and he didn't care. Someone would ease him up, as gently as they could given that doing so caused him obvious pain, and someone else would try to trickle soup into his mouth. Who these people floating round the bedroom were, he had no idea, except... Phil was there, a calm, disembodied voice issuing instructions. Raith was there too—he was sure of it—and he had a paintbrush instead of a spoon in his hand. He must have been dreaming. At some point, he *was* dreaming. He was in jail. He was standing on a chair. He was bloody and beaten and scared and crying—and that's when he woke up screaming "Ross!" The relief he felt when Ross came running into the room was immense, no, immeasurable. He let himself be held and, although it hurt his ribs, he sobbed like a child. Then, still sitting up and wrapped gently but firmly in Ross's arms, he fell into a deep but natural sleep, not one induced by whatever they'd been stuffing into him and, gradually, he got stronger.

* * *

Raith *had* been there in Angells' room, often. So had Phil. Phil had stitched him, cleaned and dressed his wounds, kept him drugged and watched over him as carefully and as tenderly as he would have done had Mike Angells been a baby. Raith, instead, had painted him, and, three months later, when Ross put on Raith's latest show, Raith had three new "Angells" to display.

One was a typical nude, replete with flowers draped strategically. Ross suggested they entitled it *Out of Reach*, an allusion to their lover's unavailability—to anyone but themselves, that is. The other two were rather different. The first was simply called *Bruised*. Angells had been right: Raith had been there with brush in hand, not soup spoon, in the days following his beating by the super. As the bruises had begun to develop, Raith had taken advantage of the morning light in the little bedroom to paint a picture of Angells' battered torso in a myriad of pinks and purples, yellows and blues. The result was a running commentary on the manner in which the bruises altered colour over time, with hues superimposed and metamorphosing into each other. The painting was dynamic: it almost looked alive and Ross was enthusiastic in his praise of it.

The remaining piece was called *The Hanging*. It was a brutally realistic portrayal of the images from which Angells found it impossible to escape. All three of his lovers had lain with him or sat by the bedside sharing the pain of his delirium, and Raith had painted his sufferings.

* * *

Ross

Raith's a strange mix. Most of the time, he's full on. Boundless energy. Tires me out just watching him. Amazing what a diet of bread, cake and chilli flakes can do! (Or perhaps that's the reason.) He throws sacks of clay around as though they weigh no more than a feather—a powerful, masterful guy. And yet, he has the most delicate touch. When he's focused on his work, when he's totally absorbed in what he's doing, he's like a different person, and what he produces can be astonishingly beautiful. Sheer artistry. Screws my emotions into knots. You can tell that he has a specific person in his mind and all the feelings he has about that person are transferred to his canvas or his clay. It used to be Peri. Now it's Mike. Sometimes Phil, but I'd say that Phil's calmness and steadiness hit a different set of feelings. Not those that need art for expression. Nor those that need hard sex for their outlet.

I suppose that Mike releases the animal in Raith whereas Phil restrains it. For example, Raith likes to paint water as it tumbles over rocks. He loves to sit by the waterfalls that cascade down the becks. I think he sees his own struggles and unease in their turbulence. Phil can smooth Raith's rivers even when they're torrents in flood. He gives him peace. Sometimes, you can actually see Raith quieting (is that a word?) when Phil's with him.

If Mike is Raith's caffeine, then Phil's his barbiturate. This is the real beauty of a lifestyle like ours. (I'm admitting it. I'm a monogamistic polyamorist!) We don't have to be all things to anyone, but between us, we can be everything to everyone.

Chapter 15

The afternoon of the show approached.

"You will come, won't you?" Raith had asked Mike.

Angells had sighed but agreed. Ross had already told him that the super would probably be there. Not just an amateur painter, Mrs Flaxby was herself an amateur ceramicist—and not a bad one either. She usually came to see Ross's productions, and both her and her husband's names were on the guest list for the preview. Ross could hardly stand duty all evening, ready to snatch his lover out of Flaxby's clutches should Flaxby wish to clutch, but Phil had said that he'd stand guard, if guarding were required.

The four men might have felt less apprehensive had they been flies on the Flaxbys' wall the previous weekend.

The Flaxbys were eating an evening meal together, a rare occurrence.

"Clive," said Mrs Flaxby between the hot pot and the trifle, "I was hoping we'd go to the Angel Band show next week and, also, you know I booked a weekend in Tunhead?"

He nodded.

"It's in three weeks' time," she continued. "Obviously, I don't know the details about Mike, but if you'd rather I cancel, then of course, I will."

"No. Go ahead," he said.

"Are you sure? I don't want to make things awkward for you. Or for me. For anybody."

"No, Dot. I know you were looking forward to going to the show and to the activity sessions. You go." He paused. "Look, I'll tell you something of what happened."

"You don't have to, Clive."

"I probably do. If only because, if they say something, you won't be in the dark."

She looked aghast when her husband finished explaining. "Oh my goodness. That's terrible. So you don't know what it was Ross did?"

"No, and I don't want to know."

"But you didn't make Mike resign? He resigned himself?"

"He knew he had to."

"And you beat him up? Where was I?"

"At some meeting or other. Why? Would you have tried to stop me?" he asked.

"No. I think I understand why you did it, but… oh Clive, that's terrible," she repeated.

She stood up and took the trifle out of the fridge. The two of them sat there, looking at it.

"What would you do, do you know? If you ever had to make that kind of choice?" she asked.

"It wouldn't happen, would it?"

"No, but what *would* you do?"

"It's hypothetical. What would you expect me to do?"

"I suppose I'd *expect* you to choose the job, but I'd *hope* that you'd choose me, even though you'd probably have to live with guilt for the rest of your life."

"Aye," he said. "Mike would understand a sentence like that." He smiled sadly. "That trifle's going cold."

* * *

The big day arrived. Phil had stationed himself near Raith's painting *Out of Reach*. Not out of reach for him, it amused him to think. He enjoyed eavesdropping on the conversations of those who weren't in the know, and it pleased him to hear that his Mike tickled the fancy of many visitors. Of both sexes too, he noted.

The real reason for stationing himself so proprietorially near that painting was not so self-centred, though. He could see the door. He'd know when Flaxby arrived and had decided that, if Mike should need assistance, he'd be on hand to provide it. With what, precisely, he didn't know. One of Raith's sculptures over the superintendent's head if necessary, though not one of the costlier ones obviously.

Angells himself was understandably nervous but had decided that avoidance was the best strategy. He'd taken a glass of white wine—a fancy plastic container made to look like glass—from a tray offered to him as he'd entered, and he'd drunk the contents slowly and unenthusiastically. As no one had passed with another tray, he simply kept hold of the glass. He saw the Flaxbys come in, and he followed the super's progress round the room, mainly by looking at the super's reflection. He knew that Flaxby had stopped for some time in front of Raith's painting of his bruised body, and he watched him spend even longer looking at *The Hanging*.

Someone spoke to him. He turned to answer but lost sight of Flaxby in doing so. Then there he was. Directly in front of him. He felt his pulse skip. He couldn't look the super in the eye.

"Sir," he said quietly and turned to go.

"Stay, Mike," said Flaxby gently, preventing Angells from escaping by placing a hand firmly on his shoulder. Angells froze.

Flaxby nodded in the direction of *The Hanging*. "So that's still what you see when you close your eyes at night, is it?" he asked.

"Yes, sir," Angells answered quietly. "And often when I open them in the day."

There was a pause.

"You got it right then, did you?" asked the super. "Look at me, Mike. The sentence? You got it right?"

Had he really called him Mike again, affectionately? Surely there couldn't be any reconciliation, not after what had happened? Slight hope warred with the certainty that, in Flaxby's eyes, he would always be an object of disgust.

Angells sighed and forced his own eyes to meet the super's. To his amazement, he saw only kindness there.

"The sentence? Did you get it right?"

"Bang on, sir," said Angells.

"Bang on, eh? Thought so. *You'd* know what punishment fits, and *I* know *you*, you see."

And then Flaxby had gone to talk to someone else. Angells leant against the wall, closed his eyes, and offered up thanks to whatever deity might have been listening to his prayers. He knew then that Flaxby might never be able to forgive him completely for what he'd done but, equally, he knew that the man had understood why he'd had to do it—and at what cost.

Phil had been tempted to rush over to Angells' aid the moment he'd seen Flaxby touch Angells' shoulder. *"Unhand him, sir!"* had popped into his mind. However, he waited, walked slowly over and opened with what he hoped was a well-disguised face-saving gambit.

"Mike," he said in as pained a voice as he could muster, "something in that buffet's really done my stomach in. Ross and Raith can't leave, obviously, but would you mind leaving and driving back to Tunhead? The others can get a taxi."

"Aye. If you like," said Angells suspiciously.

"Well go and say ciao while I get our coats," said the doctor, "and give me whatever it is—or rather, was—you're holding. You seem to have squashed it to smithereens."

"Bloody hell," said Angells as he looked at the remnants of plastic in his hand. "Glad it wasn't glass."

Phil was puzzled. That had been spoken almost as lightly as a joke.

* * *

By the time all four men had returned to Tunhead, the sun had long set. The skies were clear, though, and a full moon, albeit high and therefore looking small and lost, cast sufficient light to see by for those who knew the moorland tracks. Angells said he'd enjoy a walk up the beck and over the fells. "If your stomach's better. That's if it was ever bad," he said to Phil.

"Ah, well. Not taken in, eh?" Phil replied, laughing. "It seemed a fitting excuse. The bilious effect of worrying about you and your Superintendent Flaxby. But, no. Raith looks just about worn out." Raith nodded. "So I think he and I'll just go back to his place. You two go if Ross can manage it."

"I'm still buzzing and high as a kite," said

Ross. "I'll come up with you. Give me a minute to change."

As the two men made their way along the tracks above the village, with only sheep for company, Ross asked, "What was that he was saying about excuses?"

Angells explained.

"I can think of several non-gastrinal excuses," said Ross and, for the first time in what seemed a very long while, the two men relaxed and began to laugh.

"Tell me one," said Angells.

"We've got to go home… to cut the grass," began Ross.

"Chop the firewood."

"We're all electric."

"What if there's a power cut? Clean the windows."

"Wash the car."

"Wash the bike."

"Enough of cleanliness. Shear the sheep."

"Sheep? We don't have any sheep!"

"Milk the cow then."

"Gather the goats."

"Change the sheets."

"Iron them."

"Iron the sheets? We don't do that, do we, Mike?"

"We can always begin. I can, anyway. If you did it, they'd end up more creased than they started. Still your turn."

Still laughing and admittedly puffing a bit, they reached a bare stone outcrop that was a favourite resting place. Tunhead itself was hidden by the steep ground that rose above it, but much of the valley and Tun Beck itself dropped away below, still in moon-shadowed view.

"I love it up here," said Mike. "It always feels so peaceful."

"Sheep turds, rabbit droppings, pot holes precisely the right size for breaking ankles in... yes, wonderful," agreed Ross with mock sarcasm. "Especially in the dark. So glad I moved here and left the delights of the city behind! But yes, you're right," he added. "It is peaceful. Good for the mind."

There was a long pause, both men lost in thought.

"I let everybody down, didn't I?" said Angells, breaking the silence, "but the person I let down most was myself. Even if other people could forgive me completely, I won't be able to. That's guilt I'll always carry." He paused. "But I have to try to live with that. It would be wrong not to live with it, if that makes sense... I broke the law. I have to pay..."

"Always the policeman," murmured Ross.

"But I think the future changed course earlier today."

"What happened, love? I saw him talking to you. I wanted to ask, but I knew you'd tell me when you were ready to and not before."

"I think... I *know* he took me back," Angells said. "Not back to the job, obviously. That's gone forever, and I know that. God knows I'll miss it! But back in a personal way. Back in the fold. He took me back. I know it."

"I'm glad, Mike. I really am." Ross took hold of Angells' free arm and held it tightly with both hands. "So, the future?"

The future...

The euphoria Mike had felt at his reinstatement in Flaxby's good books faded.

His body soon regained its strength, but,

jobless for the first time in twenty years and unaccustomed to filling his day with little more than routine trivialities, he felt dejected and depressed. He knew he wanted to work, but doing what? Security? Private investigation? He fancied neither. Construction work again? Where? Not within a radius of thirty miles, and anyway, he wasn't certain if he would be welcome on a building site. There'd be too many things he would have to keep quiet about.

He didn't regret for a moment the choice he'd made. He'd do it all again, but the knowledge failed to lift his spirits. He felt as lacking in life as the scene that met his eyes as he stared listlessly out of the kitchen window: a leafless, cheerless garden under a leaden, grey sky. Spring came late to Tunhead. Not even the promise of an evening with Ross to cheer him up. Nor one with Phil. Not that he wanted cheering up. He deserved to feel the way he did.

He saw Raith walk across the garden, saw without seeing him in a sense, registered the ring of the doorbell and, without enthusiasm, opened the door to let Raith in. That single act, more than any other, sealed the future.

* * *

Raith

I took advantage of him. He'd never have let me take him the way he did if he hadn't been so unhappy. From the moment Peri left, Mike, Ross and Phil had been clear about the boundaries. Angel Baby could fuck me, but if I fucked him there'd be trouble. It was understandable. Phil sometimes described the gory details of his job to us. Child's play to Angel Baby, who must see much worse things (but never tells, except in dreams), but Phil's stories turn Ross's stomach, and mine too. So I could paint pictures of Mike naked and sculpt figures of him naked and use my hands and my mouth how and where I wanted, and he could top me if we both wanted (which occasionally we did), but the only place for my ten-inch cock was inside Phil—if *he* wanted, which he did because I'm so irresistible!

It was different with Phil. Unlike me, Phil didn't live next door, and I think that they all thought that I might muscle in too heavily, me never knowing exactly when to put a brake on things, but I did stop myself, and I kept to my side of the sword, so to speak. For a long time, anyway.

I knew Ross was away, and I wasn't expecting Phil, so I rang the bell and waited. Mike took a while to answer. He put the kettle on and he just stood there, hands on the worktop, waiting for the water to boil. I went and stood behind him, and I ran my fingers down his sides, and he tensed and he waited. I pressed him against the kitchen unit and held him tighter, and I started to kiss his neck. He didn't push me off. He didn't encourage me. It was as though he didn't care what happened anymore. Didn't care what *I* did. Didn't care what *he* did.

The kettle switched itself off and he didn't pour the water into the pot. I turned him round and unbuckled his trouser belt. I undid the stud in his jeans and unzipped the fly, and still he just stood there. I put my hand down his pants and groped him, and I knew I could take him, and I did.

In my dreams—in my imagination that is, not in sleeping dreams—making love to Angel Baby was always something really loving and romantic. Taking my time, you know? I'm big: I've got to go carefully. The reality wasn't like that at all. I was rough with him.

I shoved the whole lot inside him, and I didn't try to help one fucking bit. Then he cried. I don't mean big sobs or anything, and not because of any physical pain. The pain was in his head. I stood there and watched him blink back tears. I felt so fucking bad and mean that I'd hurt the thing I love, that instead of soothing him and telling him I was sorry, I punched him and yelled at him to shut up. Then he did fight to stifle sobs, and he looked at me and I felt that I could see all the world's hurt and misery in his eyes.

Such wonderful eyes. Such wonderful colours. Half of them I wouldn't know the names of. I've never even tried to paint them, even though I'm that tetra-thing. I've never felt I'd get them right.

I knew I'd take him again. It wasn't that he couldn't bear his guilt and he wanted to be punished. It was more like, well, just deep unhappiness, I suppose, but it wasn't meant to have been like that. Yet the more I mistreated him, the more I loved him. I love him so much that it's almost unbearable at times.

I didn't stay the night. I left him lying naked on the bed and went back home. I had a half-finished painting of him standing on an easel in the studio. I slung a pail-load of dirty water at the painting, screaming I was sorry. Then *I* cried.

We've both worked through it. We sat down one evening soon after that first time and talked to Ross and Phil about the way he'd felt and the way I'd felt and how he'd felt so miserable that he'd let me fuck him when I wasn't supposed to and stuff, and they were great. The strange thing was, once we'd talked it through with the others, neither of us seemed to need to do it. Not in that harsh way, anyhow. It's good now. I help him through it, and it's loving, and it's good.

When Peri came back, tail between his legs, begging for us to try again, I told him no, to fuck off home, I'd got everything I wanted on the doorstep. I knew from what he said that he wouldn't let it lie. The painting of the garden: that was me telling the others that I was scared of what Peri'd do.

I was right to be scared.

Chapter 16

Time dealt very differently with the two men who featured most in Raith Balan's life. Mike Angells was, by nature, a happy, positive-thinking soul. The weeks immediately following his resignation had pushed him into real misery, but his spirits were rising again. He experienced his daily dose of guilt. Nothing would alter that, and he could feel careworn and anxious, and he frequently allowed introspection to cause him to question his motives and actions, but self-analysis would pass and equanimity return. Moreover, he was fit again. He was weathering well, but then, he took steps to ensure that he did so—several hundred of them, uphill, almost daily, running over the fell above the hamlet. He was strong and lean and tanned and full of zest for living, a picture of mental and physical health, but Peri... Peri wasn't.

In his twenties, Peri had been, in Raith's eyes, beautiful. He'd still been lovely when, three years ago, the two of them had had the fight which ended their relationship. Tears, words, threats, punches thrown and kicks landed, and all because, according to Peri, Raith spent more time looking at Mike Angells than at him, and Raith was going to have to choose. Which he did.

The Peri who returned was bloated, a dull pallor adding an unhealthy wash to his olive skin.

His eyes, once bright and lively, looked bloodshot and tired. He'd put on weight and it didn't suit him. He'd made some sort of effort to impress. His clothes were smart, expensive looking and well cut, but the man wearing them hadn't simply aged, he'd aged disastrously. He looked as though he'd spent the last three years hunched in a dark corner of some smoky Paris basement, hardly moving except to raise tobacco-stained fingers and the next glass of wine to his lips.

Raith was shocked at the change, but although he felt sorry and, to some extent, responsible, he knew he could never let Peri back into his life, especially now that Angel Baby was so delightfully a part of it instead.

With Angel Baby, there weren't any fights. With Angel Baby, there were no verbal onslaughts that Raith knew were cruel even though he couldn't understand the words. With Angel Baby, there was playfulness and laughter, and with Angel Baby, there was love-making of a kind he'd never had with Peri, for Peri had always fucked him. With Angel Baby... He still felt ashamed when he thought back to that first time. He knew exactly what he'd done and why he'd been allowed to do it, but since then, he'd tried to make up for the pain he'd caused. The pain he always caused when they went the whole ten inches, but they didn't always, for with Angel Baby there was kissing and cuddling and explorations by hand and by mouth and even a little naughtiness when Angel Baby showed his somewhat less angelic side! So it was fun. The bottom line was that life was heavenly with Angel Baby, but life with Peri would be hell. So Raith sent him on his way.

He'd walked and hitched the ten miles back to the main road. Then he'd gone to Sunderland, purely because the first bus that stopped at the Tunhope Arms was going there. He went into a bar, bought a mineral water and a bottle of lager and took them to a table by the window. The two men talking at the table next to his shifted their chairs slightly to allow him to pass. He gazed out at the people on the pavement and at the passing traffic. The men continued their quiet conversation. The occasional word and phrase drifted across to him:

"…an extra fuckin' year in that hole…"

"…the fuckin' cops…"

"…another couple of weeks and then he'll know it…"

"…get even…"

Get even. That's what I'd like to do, thought Peri, and then he heard a name that made him want to swivel right round in his chair and join in. He listened harder. Angells?

"Angells, the bastard who got me sent down…" and then... Peri must have misheard. Something about it being easier now he wasn't a cop. Angells wasn't a cop? He must have heard it wrong. Out of practice. Too long speaking only French.

The two men got up to leave. Peri watched them say goodbye and go their separate ways. He gave them a minute then went to the bar.

"Those two men who were sitting at that table…" He pointed. "Do you know who they are?" he asked the barman.

"Why?" the barman asked suspiciously.

"Just a name. That's all," said Peri, pulling out a wad of Euros that he hadn't changed. "That's worth a lot more than English money at the moment."

The barman leafed through the notes Peri had placed on the counter.

"The dark one, I dunno him. The other one—name's Luke Babcock."

Peri walked along the street towards the railway station, half-formed ideas travelling round his brain. He bought a single ticket to Gateshead and went to the huge arts centre that contained the BOTWAC gallery. He knew Raith wouldn't be there: he'd left him that morning up to his elbows in clay. Ross might be, but what did that matter? Peri had every right to be there too. After all, in a sense he'd helped them pay for it. He wanted information. He went to the shop near the entrance.

There were prints of old pictures of himself hanging on the walls and, near to them, a section which displayed Raith's more recent artwork. None of the latter showed the model's face, but who else could it be? With a critical eye, Peri stood back and assessed the merits of their bodies. His own once slender, supple, youthful one. His adversary's powerful thighs that would grip a man firmly, biceps that would let the arms clasp tight. Strength. Angells oozed strength. So this was what Raith wanted now, was it? Sheer physicality, the man's vitality visible even in repose. Peri compared, and knew that there was no way that he could compete.

An assistant approached to place some rolled up posters in a box. She glanced at Peri, and for a moment, she failed to recognise him but then she said, "Peri? Peri! How nice to see you! Et ça va?"

"Bien," he replied.

The look she gave him suggested she thought otherwise.

"Et tu?" he asked, unable to remember her name.

"Bien aussi. Raith's not here," she said, obviously thinking he had come to see Balan and, from her tone, unaware of the details of their bust-up.

"I know. I was with him earlier this morning," Peri said, bending the truth a little to make it sound as though the meeting had lasted longer than the single minute it had taken Raith to tell his old flame to push off.

"That's lucky," she said. "He's usually in Dansett Cross the first Wednesday of the month picking up supplies."

"Yes, it was lucky. I take it these are Mike Angells," he added, nonchalantly pointing at the pictures on the walls.

"That's right. Though we're not supposed to say so. I suppose it's different, though, now that he's left the police."

"What?"

"Didn't you know?"

"No!" He *had* heard right, but nevertheless he was stunned. "I've been in France," he added by way of explanation. "When did he leave?"

"Six or seven months ago."

"Why?"

"I don't know, Peri. Didn't Raith tell you?"

"No."

"He's working in some driver training job, I think."

A customer was waiting at the cash desk.

"I've got to go. Sorry. There are postcards of Raith's last show in that box there." She pointed. "Why don't you have a look?"

Peri nodded and did as she suggested.

There were several photos of ceramics, undisguisedly erotic. Probably modelled on Angells, or Angells wrapped round Phil Roberts or, by using photographs, round Raith himself. Only one painting interested him—a postcard of a standing nude seen from behind. Definitely Angells: Peri recognised the musculature. No, there were two curious offerings there: a picture of a bruised and battered torso, and a depiction of a brutal beating. The colours in the hair, the proportions of the body... The assistant wasn't looking and, if there was a camera, Peri didn't care. He pocketed the postcards and went out to reflect and think and, possibly, plan.

The *Echo* had been online for several years now. Perhaps there'd be some reference there to Angells leaving the Force.

Peri bought a drink, another mineral water, and sat outside a cafe to Google likely words and phrases. Angells was, as is said, mentioned in despatches, but there was nothing about why he had left the Force. There were a couple of references to Luke Babcock as well. Robbery. *Armed* robbery—a man who would use a gun.

Peri took the folded postcards from his pocket and studied them. If these were of Angells, and he was sure they were, then what had happened? Or perhaps it hadn't happened. Perhaps Raith was simply using his imagination. The gallery girl had said that Angells was working, so he couldn't be the half-dead figure strung up in what appeared to be a prison cell. It made no sense.

He caught a bus over the Tyne and walked to the friend's he was staying at. It would take a lot of planning, and he'd need that Luke Babcock's help, but... yes, it could be done.

* * *

He recognised Luke Babcock straight away, though he didn't know the other man Babcock had brought along with him. It wasn't the man he'd seen him drinking with in the cafe that first time. He went to their table and introduced himself.

"Lassko? That Polish or what?"

"French." He spelt it out: "L-e-s-c-a-u-t. Peri Lescaut."

"Well, Peri Lescaut, what's your reason?"

"Reason?"

"For wanting to see the bugger's teeth rammed down his throat."

"He took something from me."

"What? Valuable?"

"To me."

"You want it back?"

"No. I just don't want him to have it."

"You're talking in riddles, man. What's it you're after? Wait a minute… Angells is… are you one of the LGB brigade? Shit!" He laughed. "Did Angells steal your virginity or something? Fuckin' hell. You are, aren't you? I'm not gettin' mixed up with a queer. Not even for Angells. Come on, Al," he said to the other man, getting up to leave.

Peri pulled a postcard from his pocket. "I want to do *that* to him," he said.

Babcock looked at the postcard and at the man who was holding it. "You're mad," he said. "That's not my kind of thing. The three of us knockin' the hell out of him and beatin' him senseless, I can do. Broken jaw, teeth, broken back and skull for all I care. Chuckin' him into the river and lettin' the tide take him. That too. This… no. Not my thing."

"You don't have to do anything. Just help me get him there."

"No? Get him where? I'm curious. What do you mean? What have you got planned?"

So Peri told him.

* * *

Gradually, life had resumed a certain normality in Tunhead. Mike began to work again, not in the police force, naturally, but for the IAM, the Institute of Advanced Motorists. It was something suggested by Mrs Flaxby when she had spoken to Raith at the BOTWAC weekend she attended. The work was voluntary and the hours irregular and very ad hoc, but it was the sort of thing that Mike would excel at: observing and advising bikers who wished to improve or freshen up their skills; and who knew what it might lead to? An examiner's job, perhaps. Moreover, she was sure that her husband would provide a carefully worded reference.

So Mike was sometimes in and sometimes out of the house and, one morning when he was in, he opened the door, bare footed, to a handgun held by a man he felt would use it. Perhaps he should have been more alert, more vigilant. With so much experience under his belt, he might have been expected to act smartly and disarm the man who stood on the porch pointing the gun at him. Slam the door shut at least. But he was taken unawares and he had neither the mental nor the physical energy he'd known six months earlier. He had no choice but to climb into the car where Peri was waiting in the driver's seat.

Peri was no fool. He'd checked and knew that Raith wouldn't be looking out of any windows. He'd be on his way to Dansett Cross to pick up materials from the shop he liked. Ross wouldn't be around either. It was his day for arranging things 'away', and the others, the painters and potters and weavers and smiths… if they saw anything at all, what would they see of significance? Mike Angells getting into a Range Rover with dark windows. So what?

Babcock got in the passenger seat behind Angells. He heard the door locks click into place, so he knew that there was no chance he'd be able to tumble out and, maybe, roll to safety. He thought about skewing the driving wheel around and forcing a crash, but barefoot, a loaded gun at his back? He'd gamble, but not against those odds. He had his smartphone with him. If he'd been wearing jeans, Babcock would have noticed it in his back pocket when he forced him to the car, but he was wearing shorts and the phone lay in a deep side pocket. He rested his wrist on his thigh so that the phone would stay in place and out of sight. He didn't see how he'd have an opportunity to use it, but even so, he prayed it wouldn't ring.

They drove down the road that followed the beck, and turned right at the junction with the 689, travelling west. They turned north again along a rising valley road, which narrowed the higher they drove. Just like his own Tun Beck really, but more remote and bleaker. They passed the winding lane that led to the Visitor Centre where geologists and nature lovers bought tickets to clamber along the side of the gorge and, after heavy rain, marvel at the sixty-foot drop of Harnell Force. One of Raith's paintings of the waterfall hung above the fireplace back in Tunhead.

Mike had ridden all over these tracks and lanes on his bike with Sam's arms round his midriff, years before, and he realised where they were going. They had to be heading for a farmhouse that lay derelict at the end of a steep, stony, nearly impassable track. It had to be the farmhouse. Other than a few old iron ore workings, there were no other buildings for miles. If he'd guessed right, there'd be a ruined sheep pen some way before the turn off for the track. He wasn't going to be a hero, not with a gun trained on his back and no shoes on his feet, but he still had some wits about him. As they approached the sheep pen, he said he needed to vomit. He pleaded with them to stop the car and let him spew up. After all, he was barefoot. He wasn't going to run off anywhere. Cursing, they stopped, pulling in by the gate near the pen. He stumbled out and, leaning over the dilapidated walls, did what he'd done in the super's office when he'd been told that Thijs Falconer had died.

Pretending to need a moment's respite and hands well hidden, he typed the one word on his phone that he hoped would bring help, added 'armed' and pressed 'send.' With the Visitor Centre close by, as the crow flies anyway, there'd be a phone mast and a signal, and if the super rightly became suspicious, then GPS would track the phone's location. He placed the phone onto a fallen block of limestone and, wiping his mouth on his shirt, returned to the car and hoped.

They drew up in front of the farmhouse.

"Put your hands together and put them in the air," Babcock ordered.

Angells winced as a length of rope jammed his wrists together. Peri grabbed a bag from the boot, strode to the farmhouse door and kicked it open.

"Now get out," said Babcock.

The room smelt musty—damp and fox urine. A few broken pieces of furniture were lying about. Charred pieces lay in the grate. Probably kids who, like Mike and Sam, all those years ago, had tried to light a fire in the old stone hearth. Momentarily, reminiscing took his mind off the day's reality. He and Sam had jumped back, laughing and cursing, when, lighting a fire, smoke had billowed back down the chimney and into the room, covering them with soot and pieces of bird nest. He remembered the long wooden table too. They'd added their initials to the lines and notches which had been carved into the wood over many years of use. There was a heavy-looking hammer on the table. It didn't appear to have been left behind from when the farmhouse owners left. It wasn't rusty. It looked new. There was little else in the room, just a couple of old chairs. Babcock sat himself down on one, the gun aimed and ready to shoot.

Some of the ceiling beams had collapsed, although others were still in place. Peri told Angells to stand beneath one and to raise his arms above his head. A rope had already been slung over the beam, a large meat hook dangling from one of the ends. Peri thrust the hook through the ropes tying Angells' wrists then yanked on the free end until Angells was at full stretch, almost on his toes. As Peri tied the free end to the heavy table leg, the rope slackened slightly, but Angells still felt as though his arms were being tugged from their sockets.

Peri pulled a postcard from his pocket, pretended to study it and looked at him. He waved the postcard at Angells.

"A print of one of Raith's paintings," he said. "I got it at the gallery the other day."

Angells had a sudden sickening realisation. He knew where this treatment was leading.

"No! No! You wouldn't!" he said. "Ah, no, you wouldn't!"

"I wouldn't what?"

He couldn't bring himself to answer. The postcard showed *The Hanging*. They intended to act it out.

Peri ripped the back of Angells' cotton shirt

open with his knife. Tied hands meant that the shirt couldn't be removed, but enough of Angells' back lay bare.

"Oh my God! Come and look at this!" said Peri. Something else Raith didn't reveal on paintings.

Babcock placed the gun on the chair and walked behind Angells to take a look.

"Jesus! A pretty princess! Or a pantomime fairy!"

He laughed at his own crude jest.

Peri viewed the thug with distaste. Not because of the joke. On the contrary, he felt the joke was very apt, particularly as he intended to have some entertainment at the pantomime fairy's expense. But his expert eye saw what Babcock didn't: that whoever had tattooed the pattern splayed across Mike's back and shoulders had followed Raith's instructions—it had to be Raith who'd designed it—to the final drop of ink. Far from looking like a pair of fairy wings left over from a box of panto props, these wings tapered towards Mike's midriff, giving the illusion that, somehow, they'd continue to the ground, as light and ethereal as gossamer. Angel wings. Almost a shame to destroy them.

"Oh look!" said Babcock, returning to his seat. "He's behind you! Make him say 'Oh no he isn't,' Peri."

"Say it."

Mike said nothing.

"Say it."

"Piss off! Aaah!"

The whip Peri held cut into his flesh. *God, that hurt.* Blood bubbled out and trickled down a wing.

"Ten years I was with Raith, then he dumped me for you. So let's do everything in tens," Peri said, and he began to count out the lashes. "I'll do it again in French, unless you want to give him some," he said to Babcock, who was still seated in the chair.

"No. You're doing fine," Babcock said, "but give him a couple of kicks where it hurts for me, would you? More my style."

"My pleasure," said Peri, who did as he was bid. "Look, he wants to vomit again."

* * *

Superintendent Flaxby was in a meeting in the Warbridge station when his mobile buzzed. He ignored it. It couldn't be any urgent police business: someone would have come in and interrupted if it had been. He was only able to check his messages a good half an hour later.

"Oh shit! Oh fucking shit!"

"What is it, sir?"

"A problem. Maybe a big one."

He pressed 'reply' and waited while the phone rang. Nothing.

"Mike Angells… I want to know where he sent this message from. Don't just stand there. Here." He threw his phone at the constable who stood closest to him. "Take the number off my mobile. Get onto it!" he yelled.

Snatches of a shouting match assailed those sitting or standing in the room outside the super's office.

"I don't want bloody tasers, ma'am. I want an ARU… I want a copter searching for a car. They won't have got there on the back of Angells' bloody bike… Then pull 'em off it… Get the Cessna in the air then…"

* * *

Peri ran his fingers across Angells' chest.

"I bet he likes to suck on your nipples," he said. "He used to enjoy sucking on mine. Let's see how tasty yours are."

He placed a hand behind Angells' back to hold him in place and licked. Angells brought his knee up hard between Peri's legs.

"You bastard!" Peri yelled and then ripped his knife through first one nipple then the other. He stepped back for a better view, studying Angells' face and bloodied torso as he might study a painting in the gallery. Pain. He was glad.

He'd brought a bottle of wine with him, and he sat on the second chair and drank half the contents thoughtfully, as though he was enjoying the finest vintage, before passing the bottle to Babcock.

"You like getting fucked, do you, Mike?" he asked after he and Babcock had emptied the bottle between them. He broke the bottle against the table edge. "Well, let's see what we can get up your backside."

Between them, the two men got Angells onto his back on the table and stretched his legs up so that his arse was raised.

Luke Babcock was a vicious thug, but as he held Angells' ankles and looked at Peri's face, he began to wonder if he wanted to be linked with this lunatic in any way. He hated Angells, no doubt about that, and he wasn't averse to dumping Angells' body in the bottom of a mineshaft or a reservoir. He hated him, not because of wrongful imprisonment as he'd maintained at the time of the trial, but because Angells' case against him had been so carefully constructed that not even the efforts of an expensive, bent defence lawyer had managed to find a crack. Angells had received a County Court commendation, and Babcock received ten years. Most of them had been spent wondering how to get even with the man who'd destroyed his street cred and put him and his brother away for such a long stretch. But this... It wasn't the kind of retribution the Babcocks of this world usually dish out. It wasn't his kind of fun, and he let go of Angells' ankles.

"Come on, man," he said. "He's half dead already. Way out of it. Not even feelin' the fuckin' pain anymore."

Angells groaned.

"Well, he's not dead yet, is he?" said Peri. "Hold his legs still, will you, Luke? I've got a use for this bottle."

But Babcock was moving to the window.

"Thought I could hear a plane, but I can't see it. Did you hear it?" he asked.

"You're imagining it."

"No. I swear I heard one circling a couple of minutes ago, and it's round again. Come on, man!" he said. "We need to get out of here."

"What?"

"Come on."

He grabbed the gun. They could both hear the sound of sirens now.

"Get Angells. Come on."

The only way out was back the way they'd driven, but with the gun and Angells as a hostage, they felt that they at least stood a chance of getting away. If they stayed where they were, they didn't. They stood him up and dragged him, naked except for his torn shirt, to the door. They heard shots and Babcock knew that the tyres of the Range Rover had been blown out. No escape now. God knows how long he'd go down for this time.

Before they reached the door, they heard

someone shouting at them through a loudspeaker. It was Flaxby.

"Babcock," he shouted. "We know you're armed. Well, so are we. Open the door. Throw the gun out and come on out yourself."

How the fuck do they know about the gun? Babcock wondered. *How do they know that I'm here?*

"Did you tell someone what we were plannin', you fuckin' fool?" he yelled at Peri. "We don't have a choice. We've got to go out."

"Don't be stupid. I'm not going anywhere. Give me the gun!" shouted Peri.

There was a scuffle, a shot, and a shriek of pain. Flaxby didn't know that a third man was in the room. He didn't know who had fired the shot nor who had been hit—Babcock or Angells.

"Get in there!" he screamed at his men.

Someone shot wildly at the first person who entered the room. The policeman fired back and shot Peri through the heart. Babcock was on the floor trying to staunch blood pouring from a wound in his shoulder. Flaxby ignored him. He went straight to Angells.

"Sir…"

"It's all right, Mike lad. There's a 'copter on its way. We'll get you to hospital in no time."

He started to raise Angells a little from the floor, where he'd collapsed when Babcock and Peri had let go of him as they fought for the gun, but Angells' sharp intake of breath stopped him. The man was in agony, red with blood and grey with shock. Flaxby laid him gently back down and turned to Babcock, who was being attended to by one of the medics.

"You can bleed to death for all I care," he said. "It's taking every ounce of effort not to leave you for the rats. The sooner you join that one"—he nodded towards Peri's obviously dead body— "the better."

* * *

Phil

So that's where we are at the moment. Déjà vu for me. The same hospital as when I first saw him. Ross is going spare. He blames himself for what's happened. Raith is going spare. He blames *him*self for what's happened. I'm going spare. They seem to think that using a surgeon's knife is akin to using a magic wand and—"Abracadabra!"—all will be returned to how it was, but it won't be.

For a start, Mike will be scarred for life, and when he wakes up, he'll find he has three fingers missing. Peri smashed his hand with the hammer. Three digits couldn't be saved. At least it's his right hand that's injured, and at least I said *when* he wakes up. I'm confident of that. Thank God he's as strong as an ox and can draw on his reserves. He'll need to. Shock: emotional, circulatory—ASD (medical-speak for Acute Stress Disorder) and Class One haemorrhage (the least serious type, fortunately). I've done everything I can, but, honestly, patching up one's unconscious lover is not something I'd recommend trying. I think *I'll* have ASD over it. My hand is usually rock steady, but I felt as though I was quivering like an aspen leaf.

One really curious thing... at least, it struck me as... no, not curious so much as sweet and sad really. Poignant. Raith has never, as I said at the beginning of this story, attempted to paint a portrait of Mike's face. At the moment, tucked up as he is beneath hospital covers, his face (plus a bandaged hand and an arm with its little infinity heart tattoo) is the only part of Mike that's visible. Raith brought in his brushes and sketch pad and paints and pencils. Ross and I are looking over his shoulder right this minute, watching the portrait taking shape, each stroke an act of devotion. It feels as though we're painting it together. An angel loved by clay. Perfect. Peaceful. Mike's eyes are still closed, but Raith is working from his memory and using his wonderful skill with colour. He's painting Mike's eyes open. I know they'll be right.

They are.

Author Profile

Fiction author Jude Tresswell was born and raised in the north of England, though currently lives in the south.

Jude says: "I came across the term 'extreme dreamer' recently and realised that it describes me. I've been an extreme dreamer since early childhood without ever having realised it! I lead a very full 'real' life, but I enjoy imagining too."

Publisher Information

Rowanvale Books provides publishing services to independent authors, writers and poets all over the globe. We deliver a personal, honest and efficient service that allows authors to see their work published, while remaining in control of the process and retaining their creativity. By making publishing services available to authors in a cost-effective and ethical way, we at Rowanvale Books hope to ensure that the local, national and international community benefits from a steady stream of good quality literature.

For more information about us, our authors or our publications, please get in touch.

www.rowanvalebooks.com
info@rowanvalebooks.com